Love Capri Style

Lynn Reynolds

PUBLISHED BY:
Tin Foil Hat Publishing

Love Capri Style
Copyright © 2010 by Linda Reynolds-Burkins
ISBN-13: 978-0615629650
ISBN-10: 0615629652

Published in the United States of America
This print edition: April 2012

Cover Design by Sandra Edwards.
Photos used in cover design obtained from Randy Plett Photographs/iStockPhoto and Altan 75/ Dreamstime.com.

Praise for *Love Capri Style*

Ms. Reynolds has the ability to spin a tale like no other...One heck of a romance.
~ Debbie Haupt, *The Reading Frenzy*

Four 1/2 Stars. Easy to get lost in this book!
~ *The Romance Studio*

5 Tea Cups and a Recommended Read! This is one book I did not want to put down, and one I desperately wanted to see more of after the ending scene. The sexual tension in *Love Capri Style* is thick and authentic. The characters are engaging, incredibly likable, and seem very real... The writing is fluid and natural... Lynn Reynolds has definitely made my recommended authors list.
~ Denise, *Happily Ever After Reviews*

Dedication

For Matt, who makes me believe in happy endings

Acknowledgements

So many people help in the writing of a book and never even know it.

As books go, *Love Capri Style* is a pretty minor affair. Written at the request of an editor who then rejected it, it was doomed to gather dust in a bottom drawer of my desk until friends from the Elements of RWA critique group convinced me to keep going with it. Elements is a wonderful group for any writer whose books have even a touch of romance in them. Most of my stories are mysteries or suspense, or even SF and fantasy. Writing a pure romance was a unique experience for me and the folks at Elements really helped me pull it together. I also have to acknowledge my new critique group, Pens Across the Miles—a wonderful supportive group of authors who encourage me to keep going even though I hardly ever submit anything for critiquing these days!

I have to single out Cara Marsi for all her great information about Capri. I've only been there through her eyes and on the Internet. Someday maybe I'll really get there. Thanks also to Ann Whitaker for being a great editor and an even better friend. Ann, I would have really ripped the zipper out, but then Amanda would've had to leave the party naked and I think that would've been a tad too conspicuous.

Thanks to Sandra Edwards for a fabulous cover for this new edition and for her help in formatting the new print and ebook editions.

And last but not least, thanks to Matt, who keeps me believing in the possibility of happy endings even when I don't want to.

~ *One* ~

Amanda was rifling through Eric Greyford's sock drawer when she heard the creak of the outer door to his hotel suite. Frantic, she dashed to the balcony and peered over the edge to the courtyard three stories below. Sounds of laughter and drunken cajoling wafted up to her. Flashbulbs popped right and left as the paparazzi jockeyed to photograph any one of the many beautiful people attending the Capri Music Festival.

As one of the most beautiful people in existence, Eric Greyford should be down there, seeing and being seen. Just her luck he'd decided to return to his room early. What if he had a girl with him? Maybe she should have considered that possibility before choosing this moment to break into his room.

She straightened and hurried back over to the dresser, glancing around the elegantly appointed bedroom. Hiding under the huge, bigger-than-king-size bed was out of the question. It sat on a solid platform frame. The closet would be trite and obvious. And jumping from the balcony would be suicide. She didn't want to please her editor that badly.

With footsteps drawing near, she slid the dresser drawer shut and smoothed down an imaginary wrinkle in her slim black skirt. As she did, she seriously wondered whether her career at Fame magazine was worth the risk she was taking.

"Well, hello." Greyford stopped short in the doorway, his tall, tuxedo-clad figure nearly blocking out the light from the sitting room beyond.

Amanda could hear the bemused smile in his husky voice.

"I do enjoy finding a beautiful woman in my bedroom. Although normally she's someone I've actually met."

He flicked on the lights and strode towards her, tossing a set of keys onto the dresser and loosening his bow tie. Mediterranean moonlight filtered into the room, accenting the sharp planes of his face and emphasizing his angular jaw line.

"I'm the concierge," Amanda said, glad she had thought the story up beforehand and even dressed the part. In actuality, she'd spent nearly an entire paycheck on bribing the real concierge to let her into the room. That had better be a reimbursable business expense.

"Ah." Greyford's raised eyebrow indicated his skepticism. Beneath the brow, a sapphire-blue eye sparkled with suppressed mirth.

"I was—um—putting some extra pillows in the room."

"How very attentive of you."

His rich baritone voice confused Amanda. For a moment, she forgot who she was supposed to be.

"Yes. Well, we aim to please."

She stepped sideways, intending to go around him and make her exit. He stepped sideways too, blocking her move. He was much bigger than she was. Not terribly surprising that, since Amanda stood at only five-five. But under the circumstances, it was unnerving.

In fact, everything about him unnerved her. The fact he towered above her was only the start. There was so much to find unnerving, from the bespoke suit that showed off his broad shoulders and tapered waist, to the sensuous smell of him—a complicated blend of cedar and some exotic assortment of eastern spices.

Those piercing ocean-blue eyes obviously did not believe one word she'd said. His full lips curled up at the corners in a not entirely friendly smile.

"I'm glad to know the *Quisisana* pays such devoted attention to its guests."

"Indeed we do!" Amanda nodded and tried to push past him. "And I must go see to some of those other guests now, if you don't mind, Sir Eric."

She didn't know if he should be called Sir. She knew his father was, but the intricacies of British titles eluded her.

Eric stroked a thumb over his chin, calling Amanda's attention to the slight dimple there and to his full, beautifully defined lips.

"Please. You must call me Eric. The title only applies to my father, a reward for his lifetime of public service. When they give out knighthoods for dallying with beautiful women, perhaps then it will be my turn. Care to help me achieve that lofty goal?"

He smiled again.

Amanda thought of a tiger baring its teeth. Except, of course, that like everything else about Eric Greyford, his teeth were perfect—gleaming white and absolutely even.

"Perhaps later." Amanda attempted a charming smile and even batted her eyelashes. That's what her editor Danielle would do, and the Greyford story had been Danielle's idea.

"Do you have something in your eye?" Greyford—make that Eric—seemed to be having a hard time stifling a laugh. So much for the Danielle approach.

"I'm fine. My contacts are a little dry. I'm afraid I must go, sir. Er, Eric."

She started forward yet again, and this time, he let her pass. Just as she heaved a sigh of relief, he reached back and caught her arm.

"The concierge is a rather round Italian woman with the slightest hint of a mustache." He spoke without looking at her, gazing beyond the balcony and into the velvety midnight sky in the distance.

Amanda cleared her throat, but he didn't give her a chance to speak.

"I may be in the publishing business, but I don't care for reporters and paparazzi going through my room, Miss—"

"Jackson," she mumbled, looking down at the plush carpet. How the hell had he figured that out so quickly? Couldn't she be some sort of celebrity groupie? Should she pretend she was? Would he go easier on her if she asked for his autograph?

"Very well, Miss Jackson. I doubt that's your real name, but it's easy to pronounce, so we'll go with that, shall we?" He turned to face her, never relinquishing his firm grip on her upper arm.

Good thing she worked out so much, or it would probably be bruised by now. "I'm afraid I'm going to have to call hotel security and have you removed."

Amanda blanched, and her stomach turned over. Danielle would have her head if she botched this assignment.

"Please don't call security." She hated the breathy, pleading quality in her voice.

Eric smirked, and the eyebrow darted up again. "Interesting. Most reporters I know would love a threat like that. An opportunity to write rude, uncomplimentary things about a celebrity is like a junkie's fix for most of them. You must be quite new at this."

"No, I'm not!"

Amanda's face reddened. She jerked her arm free of his grip. For two years, she'd been slogging away at *Fame*, but soon, even being the publisher's daughter wouldn't be enough to save her job. Especially since the publisher seemed to resent her presence on the staff, barely acknowledging her existence. Getting an exclusive, scandalous story on Eric Greyford—that was going to turn everything around for her, both in her career and in her personal life. Or so Danielle had suggested when they'd concocted the plan on their now infamous Night of Too Many Cosmopolitans.

What would Danielle do right now? *Think, think!*

"I admit it, I was after a story." Amanda did her best to turn on the charm, throwing back her shoulders to display her best assets. Fortunately, she'd worn the surplice-wrap blouse that showed off some cleavage. She hadn't intended to be seductive—wasn't even sure she knew how. But the airline had lost part of her luggage again, and she was stuck with the seldom-used items in the one bag they'd managed to recover so far. Danielle had pestered her to pack this blouse, raving about how much it flattered her figure. Maybe that would turn out to be a good thing.

"I appreciate your honesty. Among other assets."

Eric stalked towards her, his movements languid and smooth. He kept his gaze fixed on her eyes as he talked; yet, she was sure he'd noticed her pathetic attempt at distraction.

"Quite a bold move, breaking into my room."

"I didn't break in." Amanda's tongue flicked over her bone-dry lips. The tiger flashed a brief smile and leaned in a bit closer. That rich, woodsy smell filled her nostrils and made her woozy. Maybe that was his secret. Maybe the aftershave drove women wild with desire.

"You should patent that cologne," she said, recovering a bit of composure.

He let out a little breath of amusement, obviously surprised by her response.

"I believe it is patented." His blue eyes probed hers as he spoke. "There's a little *parfumerie* in the St. Germaine district of Paris. They've made perfumes and colognes for my family for about two hundred years. Give or take a decade. What's that scent you're wearing?"

She knew he was making fun of her. "Ivory soap."

He ducked his head down suddenly, before she could move away, and nuzzled his face against her neck. Amanda fought an insane urge to lay her hand on his dark head and stroke the thick waves of his hair.

"Quite interesting," he murmured, his cool lips brushing her neck. "Very basic. Exudes a natural innocence and earthiness."

He straightened as abruptly as he'd bent, his face alive with amusement. And something else, something a little bit frightening. But also exciting.

"My editor knows I'm here." That was stupid. As if he were planning to murder her and hide the body in his closet.

"Does he?" Eric purred. "That's not good, my dear. Your editor needs to have plausible deniability, or I'll have to drag him into the lawsuit along with you."

"Lawsuit?"

"Besides the criminal charges for trespassing, of course."

A chuckle rose from low in his throat as Amanda struggled to keep her face under control. She would not cry in front of this arrogant, privileged, womanizing snob. But the battle to hold back tears commanded all of her energy. There was none left over for a snappy riposte.

Greyford gave a little quizzical tilt to his head, as if disappointed by the lack of response.

"I don't give interviews," he went on. "I hardly need to, what with the fantastic tales you reporters create without ever even meeting me. And if I were to give an interview, it would be to one of my own magazines or newspapers. And I'm reasonably certain if one of them had sent you, I'd have been forewarned."

He paused and smiled. "Or perhaps not. Perhaps someone on my staff felt the need to put a girl in my room, along with the flowers."

He indicated a massive arrangement of snapdragons, tiger lilies, and birds-of-paradise sitting atop a dresser next to him. Amanda knew they came from his latest and greatest conquest because she'd read the card. *Thanks for a wild time! Kisses, Stacey D.*

Greyford slipped the card out of the arrangement and rolled his eyes once he'd read it. He tossed the card onto the dresser without further ceremony. The cad. Amanda pitied the notoriously promiscuous pop singer who'd sent them. Clearly, her days on Eric Greyford's arm were numbered.

Amanda planted her hands on her hips and took a deep, cleansing breath. She couldn't let this supercilious playboy get the better of her.

"Why date women like that if you think so little of them?" she demanded.

Oops. That had slipped out. Blurting was a particular talent of hers, especially when under stress. And standing this close to one of the sexiest men alive was nothing if not stressful.

Eric blinked several times in surprise and pursed his lips. "I beg your pardon?"

"You barely read her card."

"Impertinent little thing, aren't you? Particularly considering that you're in my room without my permission." Greyford poked his tongue in his cheek and waited for her to defend herself. "Perhaps I should call security after all."

"What, because I read the card on your flowers?" Amanda snapped.

A little voice in her head told her to shut up, but as happened all too often, she didn't listen to it. Her big story was ruined, her editor would be furious, her father disappointed again, and damn it to hell—she was wearing the pointy-toed high heels and her feet hurt. Now Eric Greyford was threatening to sue her or have her arrested? Fine, but she would not go quietly.

"You claim to want to be left alone, yet you spend every waking minute in the company of media hounds like Stacey Dakota. If you wanted to keep to yourself, you'd run with a different crowd. And if you don't like what's written about you, why don't you talk to a reporter—I mean, besides one that's in your own employ—and set the record straight?"

"I suppose you would be that reporter?"

Amanda shrugged.

A faint five o'clock shadow darkened Eric's cheeks, and he stroked the back of his hand over it absent-mindedly. His hand was large with wide fingers and neatly manicured nails. The image of him brushing that hand against her own cheek flashed through Amanda's mind.

"Yes, I can see that."

She shook herself, wondering if he'd read her thoughts. "What? What can you see?"

"Doing an interview with you." His quiet smile burst into a wide, dimpled grin. It was like the sun coming out after three days of rain. "I think a very long interview would be best. Over dinner. With a great deal of *limoncello*."

"Hey, now wait a minute—" Amanda protested.

Eric Greyford shrugged and lowered his hand. He stepped over to the writing desk and picked up the receiver of the phone perched there.

"Mi scusi. Dammi la polizia, per favore."

"Wait! Wait!" Amanda scrambled over to the table.

He flashed an infuriating, triumphant grin and spoke into the phone again, apologizing to the front desk operator for any confusion he'd caused. Hanging up, he turned towards her, leaning a hip against the desk. He crossed his muscular arms over his chest and stared at her.

This time, he did look at her breasts. And her hips and her legs and every other inch of her. He could hardly have been more thorough if she'd been stark naked. Her color rose higher as he appraised her.

"Good," he said. "Very good."

"I'm so glad you approve." Amanda wanted to crawl under a rock, but she didn't dare protest his lascivious gaze. It might be the one thing keeping her out of an Italian prison.

"Where are you staying?"

"The Loreley."

Eric looked perplexed. His kind probably didn't even know there was another town besides Capri on the island.

"It's in Anacapri."

"Ah." Eric straightened and strode away from the writing desk, walking right past Amanda. He moved with the smooth, rolling gait of a jungle cat. There was that image again. Eric Greyford the tiger, and Amanda a mouse in his paws.

Amanda followed him into the vast sitting room. The whole room was done in creamy shades of white, with a few dashes of lemon yellow as accents. Wildly impractical. They must have to shampoo the carpet every five minutes in a place like this. It annoyed her that her entire apartment back in New York would probably fit inside Eric Greyford's hotel suite.

"Do join me, Miss Jackson." Eric called to her from over his shoulder.

Remembering her awkward position, Amanda scrambled after him. She couldn't help admiring the snug fit of his tuxedo trousers and the firm, well-rounded shape they did so much to accent.

She made a little growl in her throat and clenched her hands into fists. She was not one of those celebrity groupies that read her father's magazines. She absolutely would not start worshipping this guy because he was richer than God and almost more famous.

Although she might consider worshipping him for his perfect physique.

No, no, no. Focus. She was here on business, trying to get a story. And he was the enemy. Target. Subject. Whatever.

Well, whatever he was, he had come to a halt in the center of the sitting room and turned to look her up and down once more.

"This could work out very well for my purposes."

There was an obscene purr in his throaty voice. Amanda refused to give him the satisfaction of babbling some incoherent response, so she stood before him in silence.

"Have you ever been to *Da Paolino*?"

"On my salary?"

"I'll take that as a no, then. You should enjoy it." Eric smiled. "I suspect you're a woman with strong appetites, and one who doesn't get to indulge them as often as she might like."

Amanda blushed again. She'd turned red more times in the last few minutes than she had in the previous twenty-six years of her existence.

"Is it very dressy?" No doubt she sounded like a nervous schoolgirl. "The airline lost most of my luggage."

"What size are you?"

"Excuse me?" Amanda's hands went to her hips again.

"Calm down, Miss Jackson." Eric re-crossed the room in a few quick steps, stopping inches in front of her. "When a strange woman invades a gentleman's bedroom, it's too late to be coy."

She could smell his cologne again. *What the heck did they put in that stuff?*

"Size six," she said faintly.

Eric stroked his jaw again. "I'll have something appropriate sent round to your hotel tomorrow. Are you registered as Miss Jackson, or did you use some other nom de plume there?"

"Amanda Jackson. It's my real name."

Eric chuckled. "Are you sure you're not new at this paparazzi game?"

"I am not paparazzi. I'm a serious journalist. Or I *was*, once upon a time."

Again came the upraised eyebrow and the smirk. Amanda wrinkled her nose at him and toyed with the notion of stomping her high heel down on his foot.

Eric laid a firm hand on her shoulder. Gently but irresistibly, he turned her towards the door to the hallway outside his hotel suite.

"I'll have my driver pick you up at your hotel, tomorrow night at eight. We can discuss your journalistic aspirations then, Miss Jackson. You'll forgive me, but I've had a very full evening, and I'd like to get to bed. Alone."

"Good. Because I know I wasn't offering anything. And forget the driver—I'll meet you at the restaurant."

Amanda thrust out her chin as he reached past her to turn the doorknob with his free hand. At the same time, the hand that had come to rest on her shoulder slipped down to the small of her back. The unexpected movement was so sudden and so smooth, she shivered.

As he opened the door, Eric managed to angle both of them into the doorway. He wasn't quite touching her—except for that gentle hand on her back. But he stood so near, she could feel the heat of his body radiating out towards her.

She gazed up into his eyes and caught her breath, her heart thumping out a thousand beats per minute. She could drown in the blue whirlpool of those eyes. Eric pulled her snugly against him, a wavy lock of dark hair tumbling forward onto his forehead. His lips brushed her hair, and her legs began to wobble on those agonizing heels.

"Tomorrow night, then." He murmured it right into her ear, his warm breath fluttering a few loose wisps of her hair. "Under the lemon trees."

She closed her eyes, ashamed of her weakness, but ready and even eager for the kiss that would surely follow. A sharp thunk startled her and her eyes snapped open. The door to Eric Greyford's room had closed, and she found herself alone in the corridor outside.

"Manipulative pig!" she shouted at the door. With a grunt, she yanked off the spikey heels and padded down the hallway barefoot.

After the girl had gone, Eric made an immediate move for the sitting room's wet bar. He fixed himself a whiskey and soda and slumped onto the spacious suede-covered couch. With a sigh, he ran his fingers through his hair. Then, he flipped open his cell phone. He'd have to cancel tomorrow's dinner engagement, but his friend Franco would understand being thrown over in favor of a pretty girl. The man was an Italian, after all. As he expected, however, Franco did not let him go easily.

"This one must be very beautiful indeed," Franco chuckled. "You are never one to shirk your social obligations or slight those close to you."

Eric picked up one of the many glossy magazines littering the surface of the coffee table. "Ah, Franco. Haven't you heard that I am—and I'm quoting—a self-absorbed playboy who loves them and leaves them? Hardly the picture of reliability you paint."

"Is that according to one of your own publications? If so, you should hire new writers."

Eric heard amusement in Franco's faintly accented English.

"No, it's according to *Fame*, of course, Tate Global's flagship publication. This article is part of Peter Tate's concerted effort to scare off Greyford investors by making me appear dangerously immature."

"If your brother's music festival is a success, that should help capture a more youthful audience for Greyford publications. Then your alleged immaturity will be an asset."

"Thank you, Franco," Eric snapped, a defensive edge creeping into his voice. "I am aware of my late brother's interest in using me to create a younger, hipper image for Greyford Publishing. Why else am I spending every waking minute babysitting our star performer?"

"Ah, the star," Franco's voice made his appreciation of her obvious. "What does she think of this date you have lined up for tomorrow evening?"

"She doesn't know. But as long as I keep it out of the public eye, she won't mind."

The entire charade with Stacey Dakota had gotten out of hand. He'd been sent to keep her sober and out of trouble over a year ago, when his elder brother had first thought up the Capri Music Festival and signed Stacey as the headliner.

"Someone has to keep her on a short leash," Antony had said. "It can't be me. I have to run Greyford Publishing. Besides, you're more photogenic. And you're always boasting about how much you love adventure. Minding Stacey should be an adventure and then some."

Eric had always felt guilty about not being more involved in the family business, so he'd agreed to the project. But now, Antony was dead, and Eric had been forced into the not very adventurous role of his successor as the company's Chief Operating Officer...

"Did you hear me, my friend?" Franco's voice dragged Eric back to the present.

"Lost my train of thought for a moment," he apologized. "It's getting quite late, I suppose."

"True. Which reminds me—where did you find your new ladylove? I was with you earlier this evening, and you had Stacey on your arm then. You do work quickly."

"In fact, she was the one working quickly," Eric replied. "I found her ransacking my room."

"So you're taking her out to dinner? This is an odd English custom they didn't teach when I was at Eton."

Eric laughed. "She's a reporter, Franco. I'm not sure for whom she's working, though. That's one of the things I hope to learn tomorrow night. In the meantime, I'll have my assistant do a background check on my mystery lady."

"If the lady in question is working for Tate Global, you might pick up some useful information from her. Perhaps she's privy to their entire plan of attack for next week's board meeting."

Eric smiled at the memory of her fumbling attempts to lie to him. "I doubt she could keep any secret for very long, much less something on that level. I don't think she's very highly placed within her organization."

"Still, a responsible company officer must learn all he can about the competition."

"Precisely."

Eric and Franco shared a suggestive laugh.

"I must do my duty for the good of the family business. If that means wining and dining the pretty Miss Jackson under the lemon trees of *Da Paolino*, I shall have to endure it. And if an even greater sacrifice is needed, I'll be happy to oblige. Good Lord, you should have seen her."

"Any parts in particular you would like to tell me about in greater detail?" Franco's voice was rich with suggestion.

"Her eyes," Eric said, surprising even himself.

"Her *eyes*?"

"Very brown, they were." Eric rubbed his thumb along his jaw, once again seeing the rich, coffee-colored darkness. The biggest brown eyes he'd ever seen, with little flecks of gold near the pupil. A surprise, considering the blonde hair. He'd looked for dark roots when he whispered in her ear and found none. Either the best dye job in the world—better than any actress or heiress he'd ever dated—or else she was a natural blond. She'd worn it bound up in a high ponytail, but unruly wisps had managed to escape and frame her face like an angel's halo. He imagined pulling the elastic out of her hair, those blonde curls tumbling down for him, spilling around him as she leaned over his reclining form. Now that would be an entertaining way to spend an afternoon.

After an uneasy pause, Franco spoke again. "Enjoy yourself, Eric. But do be on your guard with this one."

Eric promised his friend he would do exactly that, and then the two made plans to meet in a few days. Eric hung up the phone and found himself still thinking about Amanda. He recalled her little lecture about his perceived mistreatment of Stacey, and he smiled. Stacey would find it hilarious when he shared it with her. However, Franco was right. He'd need to take care with this one. Her forthrightness made her a danger, because it made him want to reach out to her.

That couldn't happen. Although he regretted agreeing to the job of pretending to be Stacey's boyfriend, he certainly wouldn't reveal that secret to a reporter from a rival publication.

No. He couldn't be honest with Miss Jackson. But he could do other things with her.

He rubbed his fingers together, remembering the silken texture of her soft springy curls. In his mind, he saw again those probing, disconcerting eyes of hers. And her lush, curvaceous body, with those ripe round breasts she was so uncomfortable displaying. Last but not least, he thought of her slender legs. Those well-rounded calves had been shown to excellent effect in the black stiletto heels.

He'd taken one look at her when he'd first walked into the bedroom, and immediately he'd imagined having her in nothing but those shoes. And he would have made her love every minute of it. He'd meant what he said about her being a woman of strong appetites. He could feel it in his bones—and perhaps some other part of his anatomy too. She had a body built for pleasure. She just didn't know it yet. But bloody hell, he was going to enjoy teaching her.

~ *Two* ~

The sharp tinny ring of the hotel's telephone shattered Amanda's dreams and roused her into grudging wakefulness. She pulled an extra pillow over her face and burrowed deeper under the covers. No use. The dream had been embarrassing anyway—something to do with crashing waves and a knight galloping towards her through the surf and sand. A knight with steely blue eyes and wavy black hair. How corny could her subconscious get?

Casting aside the pillow, Amanda fumbled for the phone. "Yes? I mean, *ciao*?"

"Listen to you going all native!" Danielle's smoky voice dragged Amanda into full consciousness. "Find any hot Mediterranean pool boys to frolic with yet?"

"I'm not looking for a hot Mediterranean pool boy, Dan."

"See, honey, that's why you're so crabby all the time. Gotta take the car out of the garage on occasion, or the engine seizes up for good."

"Danielle!"

"Fine. Did you snag any racy photos? Your dad is going to be so proud when I tell him. I gotta tell you, Kiddo, I've been pulling for you all along, but I didn't think you had the ambition. How's this for your headline: *Pop Tart Dating Playboy Pornographer*? Cute, eh?"

"Brilliant. But what if it's not true?"

Danielle made a razzing noise. Amanda could imagine her poking a very sharp pencil into her updo and shrugging as she spoke. "As if anyone cares whether it's true, Amanda. If our readers wanted reality, they'd subscribe to one of Greyford's publications, not *Fame*."

Amanda squirmed at her end of the line. She sat up in the bed and noticed the dappled Mediterranean sunlight spilling across the floor next to her bed. How late was it anyway?

"It didn't go as planned." Her voice quavered a little. As editor-in-chief of *Fame*, Danielle was a powerful supporter—and an equally powerful enemy.

"I have a possible interview with the playboy, though."

"A possible interview?"

Amanda sighed. She began to explain about her new *What Would Danielle Do?* philosophy. When she got to the part about bribing her way into Eric's room, Danielle almost cried, she was so proud of her protégé.

"So did you find anything incriminating? The alleged stash of very naughty photos of all his famous former girlfriends? Those would be worth quite a bit."

"I know," Amanda admitted. "I thought I might find them, and not do any interviews at all."

That would have been her preference. At the *Lake Havasu Star*, her home prior to *Fame*,

Amanda's specialty had been writing about nature and environmental issues. Interviewing gardeners and park rangers had been easy. Interviewing famous people made her queasy.

"My little girl is growing up!" Danielle gushed. "Did you find them?"

"Um, no. But he found me."

"He who?"

"Eric Greyford. In his bedroom."

Danielle shrieked and dropped the phone. When she picked it back up, she was barely coherent. A string of babble eventually settled down to, "You're not serious, are you?"

Back in their New York office, Amanda knew heads must have been turning at the sound of Danielle's loud, raspy shouts.

"This is a disaster, isn't it?" Amanda moaned.

"Disaster? What disaster? This is fabulous! New headline: *My Steamy Night With the Playboy.* Every juicy detail of what Eric Greyford is really like. His five o'clock shadow, his cologne, his morning breath. Does he have morning breath, or does he wake up all magically fresh and minty? Does he wear boxers or briefs? Or boxer-briefs? He's pretty ripped, so I'm betting boxer-briefs. Now the women of the world will know the answer!"

"Dan, hold on right there."

"What?"

"No underwear updates. I don't do underwear stories."

"Yes, honey, so you've told me. And considering our current crop of celebrities, that severely limits your potential assignments."

"Dan, I didn't interview him. I'm going to try to talk him into doing an interview, but I haven't succeeded yet."

"You wound up in his bedroom with the guy and you forgot to interview him?" After a brief pause, Danielle gave a little snort. "Okay, I can see how that would happen. I wouldn't be thinking about journalism either if I were in Eric Greyford's bedroom. You know, he might be younger than me, but I'll bet he could teach me a thing or two about doing the nasty."

Amanda couldn't help herself; she dissolved into a fit of giggles. "Doing the nasty? Dan, you have such an impressive vocabulary."

"Yeah, honey, I do. That's why I'm the editor and you're not."

Amanda went on to sheepishly explain about getting caught rifling through Eric's things—how she'd bought off a threat of criminal charges and a lawsuit by agreeing to dinner.

"What lawsuit?" Danielle retorted.

Amanda frowned. He'd been vague on the details.

"Um, I assumed something like slander or libel or that sort of thing."

"Sweetie, you are such a babe in the woods. He can't sue us for slander or libel if we haven't printed anything. Good of you to offer the supreme sacrifice of dinner with a sex object out of loyalty to the magazine, though. I applaud you."

A little edge had crept into Danielle's voice. "You need to bring me back a story, Amanda. I don't know how much longer I can keep telling your dad what a great job you're doing when you're getting so few by-lines. He didn't build one crappy Arizona newspaper into Tate Global Multimedia by being a gullible fool."

"I know," Amanda replied.

"Now, cheer up, honey." Dan spoke more gently. "I know you've got it in you. You're a good writer. You need more enthusiasm for your subject matter."

Amanda sighed. "I don't suppose I could ask him about whitewater rafting in Nepal? Or snowmobiling in the Yukon? I could interview him about his daredevil hobbies and some of the unusual places he's visited."

When she'd worked at the *Lake Havasu Star*, Amanda had loved reading the wire service reports about some of Eric's wilderness adventures. She was no great athlete, but she wished she could see those unspoiled places he frequented. Until moving to New York and then getting the Capri assignment, most of her traveling had been entirely in her mind.

"Sweetheart, focus," Dan scolded. "That's not the stuff our readers want to know. Here's what you need to be asking yourself: What does Eric Greyford eat? What does he wear to bed? He turned thirty recently—is he thinking about settling down? Has he given Stacey Dakota a ring yet? Get the idea?"

"Yes." Amanda gritted her teeth. She got the idea all right, and it was boring her to death. "I'll do my best, Dan."

The editor sighed heavily, but not unkindly. "I know you will, sweetie. I'll talk to you again in a day or two."

Amanda hadn't realized how late she'd slept. When she rang off from the conversation with Danielle, she checked her travel clock and discovered it was noon. She scrambled into the bathroom and fumbled with the annoying handheld shower attachment in the tub. It had been a hectic week, and the hot water felt good as it flowed over her tense shoulders and down her back. She thought about her initial excitement when Danielle had assigned her to the Capri Music Festival. She'd always wanted to visit Italy, but the first blush of enthusiasm had turned to disappointment and frustration.

What a waste of time, to chase after Stacey Dakota and her playboy lover. Surely, there weren't that many people interested in a complete stranger's personal life? And yet, she knew that there were. *Fame* was the most profitable of all her absentee father's many publications.

"You're a good writer, you could go far there," her mother had said when he made the offer. "And think how thrilled I'll be when people come into the café and I tell them you've gone to New York City to write for *Fame*."

Her mother had talked as if she would be well soon, as if she would go back to her little café in Lake Havasu and pick up right where she'd left off. Amanda had taken the job to please her dying mother, but she'd stayed on hoping to make a friend out of the man whose name was on her birth certificate. Unfortunately, after a few awkward attempts at including her in various social gatherings, her father had begun avoiding her. Now, he rarely came to the New York office at all.

Amanda picked up her travel-size bar of Ivory soap. The scent jarred her, and her memories shifted to the more recent past. She felt Eric touching her hair again, leaning down and whispering in her ear. Suddenly, the mere thought of him made her red-faced with anger. He was a user like her father. She threw down the soap and shut off the tap, climbing back out of the tub.

How dare that man order her around like some hotel maid? Easy for him to threaten her with jail and smirk about it the whole time. The man was an arrogant snob who'd never suffered a day in his life. And she was to spend her evening fawning over him, coaxing him into giving her a few thousand words of wisdom on— what? Sex with a movie star versus sex with a pop singer? His pornographic photo collection? Amanda had never dreamed that a promise to a dying woman could have made her own life unbearable in so many stupid, aggravating ways.

Wrapping herself in a towel, she returned to her bedroom and sat down on the edge of the bed, gazing out at the azure sky. A fluffy round cloud caught her eye, one of the few on the horizon. Amanda could swear it had the shape of a woman's face. She'd begun to dreamily trace its outline in mid-air when a sudden sharp rap on her hotel room door made her leap up, dropping the towel as she did so. She let out an embarrassed shriek, even though no one could see her.

"*Signorina*? Are you all right?" The alto voice of an older woman issued through the door.

"I'm fine. Give me a minute."

Amanda wound the towel around her body, tucked in the flap, and went to unlock the door. Then she dashed for the bathroom

"You can come in now," she called over her shoulder. "I'm sorry, I guess you've been waiting all morning to clean this room. I got in late last night and overslept. You can start on the bedroom, and I'll get dressed in here."

"*Mi scusi*? How will I measure you if you are in the bathroom and I am out here?"

Amanda froze on the threshold of the bathroom. She spun round and found herself facing a severe woman in her late fifties. The stranger wore a silk blouse and black palazzo pants - hardly the wardrobe of a hotel maid, even on this island of the beautiful people.

"Measure me?"

"*Signore* Eric said you had no clothing, but I had no idea the situation was this severe!" The woman smiled at Amanda, inviting her to laugh at the little joke.

"He didn't!" Amanda growled low in her throat. "He was serious?"

A part of her rose up in irritation—the man wasn't even here, and he was trying to control her. But another part found room to be complimented. She'd told him she'd lost her luggage, and he'd said he would send someone with a whole new wardrobe. A girl could get used to that sort of attention. Maybe too used to it. Once withdrawn, that attention would be difficult to forget and even more difficult to live without.

"Tell Mr. Greyford that's very thoughtful, but I can't accept his hospitality."

The woman looked crestfallen. "But you would be such a pleasure to dress! You are not very tall, but you have lovely proportions—a real womanly body, not like so many of the other ladies *Signore* Eric dates."

With some effort, Amanda ignored the dressmaker's diplomatic allusion to her own too-ample figure. "Geez, do you dress them all for him? That's a little creepy, don't you think?"

The elegant lady peered over the top of her large black-framed eyeglasses. Her look indicated she found Amanda's line of questioning to be a trifle too forward. "I am *Signora* Claudia Ponti. My family has served all the fine ladies who come to this island for many generations. They come to me on their own, *Signore* Eric does not need to send them."

"That's impressive," Amanda replied. "But I'm not one of them, and I can't afford you."

"Ah." The woman's face softened. "An admirable show of self-sufficiency, but the *signore* was prepared for that. I am to tell you that he does not want to be embarrassed by you at dinner tonight. Please do not show up in blue jeans in some misguided attempt to prove your independence, he says."

"He says that, does he?" Amanda thrust her hands onto her hips and bit her lower lip. "How about if I don't show up for dinner at all? He wouldn't have to worry about my embarrassing wardrobe then."

"No, *Signorina*," the dressmaker agreed. She folded her hands in front of her stomach and waited, the perfect unflappable servant.

Amanda nearly dismissed the woman, until she recalled her conversation with Dan. *You need to bring me a story.* And Dan was right—dinner with Eric Greyford would be quite a story, possibly worthy of the front cover. Possibly even worthy of a small morsel of approval from that stranger she rarely called "Dad."

"Fine," she sighed. "Can I put on some underwear before you start measuring things?"

"Did you get my flowers?" Stacey Dakota asked in her squeaky Peppermint Patty voice.

Seated beside her at a sunny table in the town's *Piazzetta*, Eric frowned. He'd forgotten the flowers. Amanda Jackson had called them to his attention last night, but his mind had been otherwise occupied.

"Why, yes, I did." He smirked. "Wild time, indeed. What would the paparazzi think if they saw that card?"

"What they're supposed to think," Stacey reminded him. "I thought it was pretty clever."

Eric cocked an inquisitive eyebrow at her. "How so?"

"I had a wild time. The zoo. Get it? We went to the zoo in Rome before we got here, and I had a *wild* time! Get it?"

She poked him in the side with her elbow. Eric stifled a laugh and pretended to be irritated with her. She gulped down a mouthful of orange soda and hiccupped. After a few seconds, she spoke again. One thing Eric had learned long ago was that Stacey could barely go three minutes without filling the air with her voice.

"Hey, know what? I think Franco Battali likes me." Stacey had the giggle of a little girl, high-pitched and bubbly. In many ways, she was twenty-three going on sixteen.

Eric tugged his sunglasses down a bit so she could see his eyes when he spoke. "Of course he likes you, Stacey. That's the whole reason we're holding the festival here. My brother organized an entire music festival, and then strong-armed the selection committee into inviting you to be the headliner. All because he and Franco liked you so very much. And because Franco wants to have sex with you, not unlike three-quarters of the male population of the planet, he volunteered to host the festival on the grounds of his estate here. Positively chivalrous, he is."

"Well, you gotta admit, that's a pretty impressive level of devotion."

"A bloody psychotic level of devotion, that's what it is," Eric retorted, settling his glasses back in place. His eyes watered from the intensity of the noonday sun beating down on the *Piazzetta.*

"Come on. It's neat, Ric." Stacey had that bizarre penchant of some Southern Americans for inventing nicknames for everyone of her acquaintance. Eric had been shortened to Ric long ago. No doubt Franco would soon become Frank, or something even more absurd.

"Did you say *neat?* Who above the age of twelve says *neat?*"

"I do beg your pardon, sir." Stacey answered him in quite a respectable upper crust British accent. "Mr. Battali's level of attention is most gratifying to me."

She giggled and took another unladylike swig of her soda. A few yards away, Eric glimpsed a touristy-looking couple eyeing their table and knew they'd have to move soon. No doubt, they hoped to catch him in the act of snogging his celebrity sweetheart. Thinking the word "snog" in connection with Stacey made him laugh out loud. He swallowed it down and covered it with a fake cough.

The touristy couple—Americans, judging by their baseball caps—headed in Eric and Stacey's direction.

"I think we need to move along now." Eric caught his companion by the elbow and led her away from the table, towards an avenue lined with elegant shops and cafes.

Stacey carried her soda with her and continued to sip at it. A few yards into their walk, she pointed her straw straight ahead.

"Hey, look at that!" she exclaimed. "A lemon dress. Isn't it gorgeous?"

Eric dropped her elbow, snapping to alert like

one of his father's hunting hounds. His eye followed where Stacey pointed, picking out a raven-haired woman in a yellow sheath. Only then did he admit to himself that he'd been looking for Amanda all morning. Stacey's comment had called up a vision of her in a lemon-covered sundress Signora Claudia had shown him that morning. He'd stopped by her salon after breakfast and asked the dressmaker to personally send it, along with several others, over to Amanda's hotel.

"That's just some woman in a yellow dress," Eric muttered in irritation.

"Duh, yes." Stacey rolled her eyes. "What other color would it be? But isn't it gorgeous? I cannot wear yellow, I swear. I look like I have jaundice whenever I do."

Eric frowned down at her. "How fascinating."

"Boy, you are in one crappy mood today, buster," Stacey sniffed.

"Have I expressed to you my fondness for your peculiarly American vocabulary?" Eric took off his sunglasses and smiled into Stacey's freckled face. The freckles were usually covered by makeup or airbrushed out in publicity photos, probably because they made her look even younger than her twenty-three years.

"You sure have, pardner." Stacey's answer came with an exaggerated Texas twang. "Glad I can impress you."

Eric laid a hand on her back. "You do impress me, Stacey."

He hoped his sincerity carried in his voice. When he and his brother had met her a few years ago at a party, Stacey had been a chronic drunk and near suicidal. Her career had been heading for a downward spiral by the time Eric's brother enlisted her to appear at the festival. Antony and Franco held Stacey's music in much higher regard than Eric, who preferred classical or jazz. But he liked Stacey. She had an underlying native intelligence that might just save her from the greedy self-interest of her parents—or The Management, as she referred to them.

In the past year, Eric had done his best to get her sobered up, and she'd done better than he'd expected. He realized now that he'd made Stacey a charitable project, a mission to focus on in the wake of his brother's sudden death ten months ago. Now that the festival was a few days away, though, Eric found he had mixed feelings about Stacey's progress. A brotherly pride in her comeback warred with a genuine fear that Stacey was too emotionally delicate to stay in show business.

Stacey shifted under his hand, looking away from his intense gaze. "Man, you're not getting the hots for me after all this time, are you?"

Eric shook his head and laughed. "I wouldn't dream of it. Let's go and get a gelato."

He threw an arm across her shoulders in a playful headlock, and Stacey heaved an exaggerated sigh of relief.

"You and the gelato," she muttered.

They strolled down the *Via Camerelle* together, planning what Stacey would say and do in the television interview she had scheduled for later that afternoon. Eric kept his arm around Stacey's shoulders, and they walked with their heads close together, so that they could keep their voices low.

As they entered the perimeter of the little outdoor *gelateria*, a glint of sunlight reflecting off glass flashed in the corner of Eric's eye. Looking over Stacey's head, he spotted the source—a photographer seated at one of the tables and changing the lenses on his camera.

Sensing he was being observed, the photographer glanced up and spotted Stacey. He lunged towards them.

"Can I get a photo, Ms. Dakota?"

Stacey laughed out loud, but Eric was caught in mid-frown. No doubt the unflattering image would be prominently featured in Fame's next issue. Eric had seen the scruffy cameraman at a host of other events and knew he worked for Tate Global. Snapping away, the photographer followed in their footsteps. Eric hated these moments. He'd experienced a modicum of celebrity as the handsome son of Sir Lucas Greyford, but nothing on the level of what Stacey endured daily. Traveling in her orbit could truly exhaust a man. Yet much of the time—now, for example—Stacey thrived on the attention. She beamed at the cameraman, striking a few playful poses.

Eric released his hold on Stacey and stepped up to the gelateria counter.

"Doesn't try to avoid the glare of the spotlights, does she?" came a tantalizingly familiar voice.

Looking to his right, Eric found himself face to face with Amanda Jackson once again.

She was wearing one of his dresses, one Signora Claudia had shown him this morning. A little knit slip of a thing with V-shaped stripes down the front. One of her bra straps peeked out from beneath the strap of the dress, and Eric could barely resist the urge to reach over and shift it back into alignment.

"No, she doesn't," Eric admitted.

As he spoke, his mind raced, wondering what it meant that Amanda was wearing one of the dresses he'd sent over. It could mean she was pragmatic and practical, the sort of girl who never refused expensive gifts no matter how she felt about the giver. Stacey was like that; he doubted Amanda was the same. Had wearing his gift excited her? It excited him to see her in it. He scanned her up and down, noting how the dress skimmed her generous curves. She wore black sandals with ankle straps, which called attention to her shapely, tan legs. He envisioned himself stroking his hands up their silky smooth length, coming to the hem of her very short skirt and going farther, touching all her hidden places, feeling the moist heat of her.

"Melon-kiwi, Signorina," said the rotund man behind the gelateria counter.

"*Grazie.*" Amanda turned away from Eric and retrieved her cup of gelato.

In his turn, Eric ordered a chocolate-hazelnut for Stacey and another melon-kiwi.

Amanda had stepped off to the side but remained near. Her eyebrow shot up in amusement.

"Copycat," she teased.

"Not at all," he told her. "It's my favorite."

"Mine too." Her face turned an attractive shade of pale pink.

Eric was delighted that a woman could blush simply because they both liked the same flavor gelato.

"Your girlfriend gobbles up the spotlight," Amanda added.

Eric's jaw twitched as he resisted the urge to correct Amanda's choice of word.

"She does, at that," he admitted. "I can't say I enjoy it nearly as much."

"Come on." Amanda's lips parted in a flirtatious smile. "You were already pretty famous."

"Nothing like this," Eric insisted.

The rotund man brought him the two cups of gelato. Eric handed over his money and stepped away from the counter. Amanda fell into step beside him, heading towards the table occupied by the bearded, shabbily dressed photographer.

"Is he yours, then?" Eric asked.

Amanda gave a short, sarcastic laugh. "You make him sound like my pet sheepdog."

"Isn't he?" Eric squinted. "Wait, I see. He's a photographer. I often have difficulty telling the two breeds apart."

"He's a breed apart, all right. Zeke Brennan. Ask him about his Pulitzer for war photography if you want to pass a couple of hours."

Eric eyed the man with some surprise, wondering how he'd gone from serious photojournalism to snapping candid shots of celebs eating ice cream for *Fame*.

"You two work together, then?"

Amanda cast an amused sidelong glance at him. Did she suspect him of being jealous? He only wanted to know who her employer was. He hardly knew her well enough to be jealous.

"Hey, Ric, where's my gelato?" Stacey motioned him over to the table.

"Ric?" Amanda's smooth voice oozed with distaste.

Eric shrugged. An unfamiliar wave of embarrassment stole upon him. "Apparently, people from Texas are required to nickname everyone."

"Poor you," Amanda retorted. The tiniest bit of heat smoldered in her voice, suggesting the two of them were in on some naughty secret.

Someone spoke to him as if from a great distance. He blinked and tore his gaze away from the promise in those dark eyes.

"Isn't that right?" Stacey's face was alive with sly amusement as she glanced back and forth from Eric to Amanda.

"I'm afraid I wasn't listening to you. Darling." Eric fixed his gaze on Amanda. Her spoon wavered above the cup of ice cream, and she ducked her head down.

"I said, we need to be on our way, don't we?" Stacey repeated, linking her arm through Eric's. She turned her attention to Amanda, who'd sat down beside the scruffy, bearded photographer. "I'm doing a television interview, and I'm trying to start being on time for things."

"One quick shot of you with the future Mr. Stacey Dakota," the photographer quipped.

Eric glared at the man as he snapped off a series of quick shots.

Amanda laid a hand on her companion's sleeve. "Put it away, and let them go, Zeke."

Eric didn't know what disturbed him more—being called "Mr. Dakota" or being defended by Amanda because of it.

Stacey twiddled her fingers at the photographer. "We really have to leave."

She wrapped her hands around Eric's arm and tugged him backwards. "Come on—honey. We don't want to be late."

Stacey's harsh, coppery highlighted hair glared in the sunlight as the couple hurried away. Amanda's insides turned over at the sight. What did he see in that empty-headed pop star—

a handsome, sophisticated man like Eric Greyford? And what did it mean, that he would look at her in the way he had, with his girlfriend standing right beside him?

Damn it. She'd worn one of the dresses Signora Claudia had brought to her room—one of the dresses he'd paid for. She must look like a ridiculously easy target to him. She'd never have worn it if she'd expected to see him; only the turquoise and blue stripes of the dress had made her look so slender and somehow taller too. Signora Claudia had been a very persuasive saleswoman, and yes, Amanda had been flattered—too flattered. A year's salary wouldn't have covered the cost of the six dresses the signora insisted on leaving in her room. Hard not to take a liking to a man when he was willing to spend that much cash on you.

Amanda wrinkled her nose at her own line of thought. Had thinking like that led her mother to take up with Peter Tate?

"We should follow them."

At first, she was glad to have Zeke interrupt her musings. Until what he'd said registered.

"I'm not following them. They're on their way to an interview."

"Some nice lonely spots along this road up into the hills," Zeke observed. "Great places for a quick make-out session. And I've got my telephoto lens with me."

"Zeke, for Heaven's sake!" Amanda pressed her hands to her temples.

"What, what?" Zeke snapped. "That not your cup of tea? Then why are you working at *Fame*, Jackson? What do you think our readers want? Articles about some aging soap star's wildflower garden?"

Amanda closed her eyes and counted to ten. She'd been proud of the piece he mocked, but it had made her a laughingstock in the *Fame* newsroom. Dan had run it with great reluctance, cutting it to one page and burying it in the back of the magazine.

"The technique is called green landscaping, Zeke. The article was meant to be about larger issues than Mary Prentice's garden."

Zeke threw his hands up in the air and looked to the heavens. Then, he looked back down at Amanda. "A lot of folks think your father is the only reason you're still employed at *Fame*. Stories like that don't help you. And flirting with his rival won't help you either."

Amanda blew out a great puff of air. "I was not flirting. And how can people at the magazine be thinking I'm only employed there because of my father? No one but you and Dan know Peter Tate is my father!"

Zeke's fiddled with one of the lenses in his bag.

"Zeke? Did you tell people?"

Reluctantly, he met her gaze. "No, I didn't. But *someone* did. I've overheard talk."

Had Dan spilled the beans to her employees? Was Amanda doing such a bad job that Dan needed to make excuses for her presence on the staff? That was a disheartening thought, yet entirely believable. Amanda was a good writer, and she had dozens of clips from her work at the *Lake Havasu Star* to prove it. But even she had to admit her work at *Fame* hadn't been up to par. The truth was, she'd taken the job for all the wrong reasons. It hadn't led to a cuddly relationship with her estranged father. Now she hung on to the job for equally bad reasons—the phenomenal pay, the prestige, the excitement of being in New York. And still that tiny little hope that she and her father could find a way to be friends.

Zeke gathered up his camera bag and bottled water. "Look, Kiddo." He waved the water bottle in the direction Eric and Stacey had taken. "That guy was hot for you, or I'm blind. Use it. Get a story out of him, one that will impress your dad and shut up your critics. Maybe something about his plans for Greyford Publishing."

"That doesn't sound very sexy and exciting."

"No, but your dad will like it. You'll make Greyford look like a fool, since he probably doesn't have *any* plans for the company. All his plans revolve around getting girls like you naked. The guy goes through women like I go through memory cards. He's just a user."

Amanda started at the sound of the very word she'd thought earlier in the day.

Zeke uncapped his water bottle and took a sloppy gulp, the drops running down into his beard. "You need to focus on getting some good interviews, Jackson. Or Daddy—and even Dan— are gonna get fed up and ship you back out to the desert."

Zeke turned and stalked away, muttering under his breath all the way.

Amanda relaxed her posture, discovering little half-moon nail marks in the palms of her hands, where she'd clenched her fists. Zeke was infuriating, but in a way, he was right. If she didn't want to go back to her little newspaper in the desert, she needed to hustle for the big stories. And tonight would be a golden opportunity to do exactly that.

~ *Three* ~

Eric liked people to be prompt. That was why, despite the rarity of vehicles on Capri, he'd offered to send a car round for the shapely blonde reporter. He sighed heavily and drummed the fingers of one hand on the tabletop. It was foolish to sit here waiting for her. Some no name reporter from *Fame* magazine of all places.

He'd guessed her employer once he saw her photographer, recognizing the loud and overbearing "Zeke" from his numerous appearances at other celebrity events. Good Lord, he hoped she didn't bring that greasy, hairy brute into *Da Paolino* with her. Of course, that depended on whether she tried to make a news story out of this little get-together. He sincerely hoped not. He hadn't made the assignation in order to talk to her—or her slovenly photographer for that matter. No, he'd invited her to dinner for other reasons—ones having much more to do with the long, tanned legs he'd spotted in that striped dress earlier today. He decided he'd wait another ten minutes for those legs.

Maybe even fifteen.

His cell phone rang, and he snatched it up from the green and white-checkered tablecloth. The caller ID indicated it was his personal assistant in London. With reluctance, he answered, knowing it would be more tedious details about the board meeting scheduled for next Monday. He'd deliberately postponed the meeting until after the Capri Music Festival. With Greyford Publishing acting as the festival's top sponsor, success for the festival might mean success for himself at this meeting. Right now, he was acting Chief of Operations in the wake of his brother's death. He needed some way to convince the directors to make that title permanent, and the festival was his only immediate option. If it failed, so did he. The Board would undoubtedly vote in favor of selling out to Tate Global. He wasn't even sure his father would argue the point. Heart disease had put him on the sidelines at Greyford Publishing; since Antony's death he seemed to have lost all interest in the family business.

Eric's matronly assistant regaled him with minute details about board members and their expected positions on Monday's vote. "Oh," she added as an afterthought. "I looked up your young reporter."

"Did you?" Suddenly Eric found himself far more interested in Cathy's conversation. "What did you find?"

"She's been a reporter at *Fame* for nearly two years. I can email you some samples of her work there."

"Please do."

Cathy's neutral tones couldn't hide the intrigue in her next remarks. "You might be more interested in the work she did prior to her stint with Tate Global."

"Do elaborate, Cathy."

"She worked for a newspaper in Arizona, where she did columns about nature and environmental issues. I know your interest in the outdoors, Eric, and I know you have hopes of turning Greyford into a more environmentally conscious organization—"

Sometimes Cathy seemed to know more about his plans for the company than Eric did.

"She seems underused at *Fame.* It's quite a different direction for her. You might want to test the waters, see if she'd be interested in joining one of Greyford's publications as some sort of nature reporter."

Eric stifled a laugh. Amanda wouldn't feel underused in his employ. And he'd be more than happy to test those waters.

"A very astute suggestion, Cathy."

Cathy returned to the subject of the board meeting, appending a few details she'd failed to mention earlier. As his PA's muffled voice continued to issue through the phone, Eric's eyes wandered all around the crowded tables of the outdoor restaurant. Behind him, the sun had begun to sink below the horizon, casting a red-orange tint on the diners and even on the lemon trees surrounding them.

Like a goddess, Amanda emerged from the fiery light, her blond hair piled atop her head in a loose, sexy updo. Her curls glowed like a saint's nimbus, but her body swept all thought of holiness from a man's mind. She'd worn another pair of high heels—insane on an island with so many staircases and steep hills; yet he couldn't argue with the results. Parts of his body sprang into high alert at a mere glimpse of her bare legs. For a few seconds, she looked lost, and he enjoyed the opportunity to study her unawares. Then, a waiter approached her and nodded her in Eric's direction. Their eyes locked across the bustling space, and she graced him with a warm, wide smile. His chest contracted as his heart skipped a beat.

What a ridiculous overreaction. The mere sight of a woman shouldn't render him unable to breathe. He'd been too preoccupied by his new responsibilities at the company, and he'd neglected his own needs. Tonight, he intended to rectify that oversight. With a start, he realized Cathy was still speaking, had in fact, asked him a question.

"I'm afraid something's come up," he told her. "I'll get back to you in the morning."

He silenced his phone in the midst of her sputtered protests.

"I'm so sorry!"

Miss Amanda Jackson hovered in front of him, fluttering like a hummingbird. Breathless and wide-eyed, she fanned herself with both hands, doing a fine job of showing off her sleek, lightly muscled upper arms in the process.

"I took a wrong turn and wound up heading in the direction of the *Marina Piccola*."

Eric rose, noting she wore an unfamiliar salmon pink dress—not one Signora Claudia had helped him select. A little display of independence then. That pleased Eric immensely. He liked a woman with a will of her own.

The dress also displayed her assets to fine advantage. Although the boatneck collar showed not one iota of cleavage, the silky fabric clung to her curvaceous body. Her ample bosom heaved up and down as she tried to catch her breath.

"Do have a seat, Miss Jackson," he urged, stepping behind her to pull out her chair.

To his delight, the back of the dress scooped much lower than the front, revealing the sensuous angle of her shoulder blades and a smooth, golden expanse of skin. Above her zipper, the tag of the dress poked out.

Eric laid his hands on her bare shoulders and leaned in close to her. "Your tag is showing," he whispered into her ear. "Shall I fix it for you?"

Amanda glanced up and over her shoulder, her lips upturned in a skeptical grin. "I expected something more original from you."

"I assure you, I'm quite serious."

She reached a hand around her back, feeling blindly.

"Come, don't be ridiculous." Eric slipped a hand from her shoulder, sliding it down over one of those strangely erotic shoulder blades, and then rested his fingers above the edge of the garment. He slipped the tag back into place, allowing his fingers to linger for a few seconds longer.

Amanda gave a ragged sigh. "Thank you. I think."

"My pleasure." He spoke right next to her ear, so close that his lips brushed against the lose tendrils of her hair. She made a soft, high, surprised sound and arched her neck a bit, moving towards him rather than away. As she shifted, the scent of fresh oranges wafted up from her hair and neck. Eric straightened, reluctantly taking his hands from the back of her chair before returning to his own seat. "You've put on a different perfume."

"I found this place that custom makes perfume," she explained. "So I bought some. I don't know how customized it really is. They whip it up fast. But I had to do something, didn't I? I couldn't stand the idea of going on a date with a guy who smells better than me."

Her big brown eyes glittered in the fading light. In that instant, he knew he'd have to have her tonight. He wanted every inch —the wisps of blonde curls that framed her heart-shaped face, the coffee-colored laughing eyes, the firm, toned body, even the pink-painted toenails in the precarious white heels. Solid evidence of his arousal strained at the seams of his pants, and he hastily flicked open his napkin and covered his lap. For good measure, he pulled his chair a bit closer to the table.

Amanda laid a small clutch purse on top of the checkered tablecloth. Eric eyed the innocuous item with amusement. How obvious could she get?

"I'm so glad you decided to join me for this *date*." He placed a strong emphasis on the last word, and as he did so, he reached across the table and picked up the little bag.

"Hey!" Amanda cried, but he'd already opened the clasp and found the small digital recorder hidden inside.

His "date" slumped down in her seat and pursed her lips. Eric shoved aside her lipstick and cell phone and laid the recorder on the table midway between them. He eyed her with mild disdain.

"You are quite terrible at this, you know."

"Excuse me?"

"First, I catch you ransacking my room. Next, you leave the recorder where I can find it. I don't think your heart is in your job, Miss Jackson. What were you looking for in my room last night?"

Her face flushed a pale pink, the perfect complement to the deeper color of her dress. "The photos."

Eric massaged his forehead.

"You know, the ones of your, er, girlfriends."

"I guessed what you meant." Eric pushed a few buttons and erased the recorder as he spoke. "Did you seriously think if I had a collection of dirty photos I'd bring them to my hotel in Capri?"

He flipped over the recorder and popped out the batteries, fixing his attention on the machine as he spoke, not wanting to give anything away.

"My editor seemed to think maybe you'd have done a new batch of them here in Capri."

"With Stacey, you mean?"

Amanda hunched her shoulders like a child caught stealing candy. "It sounded like a possibility. I don't like trying to track down celebrities and interview them, so I thought it would be easier to find the photos and do a story about them."

Eric shook his head. "You don't like doing celebrity interviews? Aren't you in the wrong line of work?"

"Yes, I think I am. But it's taken me a while to figure that out." Amanda flicked at an imaginary crumb on the tablecloth. "Now, I'm killing time and paying the bills while I figure out what to do next, you know? Okay, I guess you don't know. It's not like you have to wrestle with what you want to do. You're pretty much where you're going to be for the rest of your life, right? Chief

Operating Officer of Greyford Publishing at thirty, and then you'll be President and CEO when your father retires. Now, that's job security."

A definite chill descended on him. The warm July night receded all around him, and he imagined himself an old man whose fate had been sealed long ago.

"Stefano!" he snapped. The maitre d' dashed over to the table. "Throw these away, will you? There's a good chap." He handed the batteries to the man.

Amanda's mouth flapped open and closed. "Those were brand new!"

"I'll buy you more." Eric's tone was curt as he tried to rein in his irritation. "Tomorrow. By the way, despite what your rumormongering magazine says, I don't take pictures of naked women. I photograph wilderness areas—the Serengeti, the Australian Outback. I was hiking in the Amazon Rain Forest when my brother died. I don't think Tate Global would be interested in those photos—not squalid enough for your company to publish."

"So have your own company publish them," Amanda retorted. "You could do one of those big coffee table books. I'd buy it. I'd love to see the rain forest. Or the Serengeti."

Eric tilted his head to one side, studying her. Difficult to tell whether she meant what she said, or why. Was she speaking to him as a woman interested in spending the night with him, or as a reporter still hoping to get a few thousand words of copy out of this dinner?

Or worse, as a corporate spy for Tate Global, trying to discern his long-range plans and thus allow Tate to somehow pre-empt any move he might make to expand Greyford Publishing's holdings? Did she know that he'd thought about taking the company into publishing books—glossy photo books, travel books, the very sort Amanda had mentioned? He'd even considered branching into producing documentaries about the environment, knowing the days of print media were limited. But as *Acting* Chief Operating Officer, he didn't dare share his vision of the company's future with the skittish board members—too many already secretly favored selling out to Tate Global. His brother's music festival idea had made them nervous enough; Antony dying in the midst of the planning had almost provoked a panicked sell-off of company stock. Eric would need to implement any new plans with extreme caution, something that had never been his strong suit. Was he being incautious in speaking to her now?

"I've considered doing that," he said, trying not to give too much away. "But that trip was cut short, and I put the project on hold. I don't know when I'll get back there. Company business takes all my time these days."

"Not all of your time. You're here, aren't you?"

Amanda leaned across the table, her nearness prompting him to make eye contact with her. Her smile brought the Mediterranean warmth back to him. Dimples accented the round fullness of her cheeks. As he studied her perfect heart-shaped face, she reached a hand across the table—and laid it on top of the disabled recording device.

Eric arched an eyebrow.

"Look, it wasn't cheap, and it's harmless now."

Eric nudged the lifeless machine in her direction.

She smirked as she tucked it back into her bag. "I could have another recorder hidden on me, you know."

Eric smiled and brought his head closer to hers, his dark hair tangling with the stray wisps of her wheat-colored locks.

"Unlikely," he whispered, offering up a conspiratorial grin. "That's an extremely tight dress you're wearing."

Amanda moved away from him, clearly disconcerted. Still, the ghost of a smile played on her lips, which were so wet and inviting. Their glossy fullness provoked a riot of carnal fantasies about where he'd like her to put those lips, and what he'd like her to do when she got there.

"Don't be so cocky, Mr. Greyford. Eric. They make some very small recording devices these days."

Eric stroked a finger over his lips, barely able to suppress his amusement at the image that flickered in his head. "I could always frisk you to be certain."

Unexpectedly, Amanda laughed out loud. Her light, throaty trill lifted his spirits. "You are incorrigible, aren't you? How does Stacey Dakota put up with you?"

"She and I have an understanding."

Eric cocked his head to one side and watched Amanda's reaction. The gleeful light died out of her eyes.

"Men who cheat always seem to think that."

For a moment, he wanted to tell her the truth, but one glance at her purse reminded him why that would be unwise. She was beautiful. She would be warm and responsive to his touch—had already responded every time he'd touched her. But he'd be wise to keep in mind that she was still a reporter.

"I don't cheat," he told her. "But Stacey and I do have an arrangement."

Amanda arched one delicately sculpted brow. "And now you're hoping to make another arrangement with me?"

Eric shook his head, mock scolding her. "Amanda, dear, the night is young," he said. "And it would be so much more enjoyable if you remained open to all its possibilities, don't you think?"

Eric could see her thoughts warring in her face, could see that although his suggestion offended her, the idea of an evening of pure indulgence intrigued her. The idea intrigued him too, as few had in this long, difficult year of transition.

"We should start with drinks, don't you think? Have you ever had *limoncello*?"

The earth rolled away from the sun, and night fell on the tiny isle of Capri. *Da Paolino* took on the quality of a fairyland. Tiny white lights strung throughout the lemon trees flickered into life, enhancing the otherworldly feel of the place. Eric and Amanda sat a little apart from the other diners in an alcove near the back of the outdoor restaurant. Amanda didn't imagine he'd chosen the out-of-the-way table because it was romantically secluded. She knew Eric's own celebrity factor had skyrocketed since hooking up with Stacey Dakota. While that might be good public relations for Greyford Publishing, it couldn't be good for a man trying to seduce someone other than his very famous girlfriend.

And seduction was obviously Eric's goal this evening. The whole dinner had been mapped out before Amanda even arrived. A first course of oysters on the half shell had been placed upon the table along with the *limoncello*. Eric had explained that he'd taken the liberty of ordering the very best specialties of the house for both of them to sample. Coupled with the business of the dresses, Eric choosing their dinner all on his own indicated a slightly scary obsession with control.

"Were you always like this?" Amanda asked as a waiter brought an assortment of small pasta and fish dishes to the table. It reminded her of *tapas* in a Spanish restaurant.

"Like what?"

"A control freak who chooses women's clothing and food for them."

Eric, who'd been buttering a slice of crusty Italian bread, froze in motion. The hand holding the knife wavered the tiniest bit before he put it, and the bread, down. His blue eyes slid away from her. Normally, that would be a sign a person was about to tell a lie. Yet it seemed to work the opposite with him. Every time he came near to saying something real, something that mattered, those cool blue eyes would shift away.

Amanda tried to assuage whatever nerve she'd struck. "It's just—before you hooked up with Stacey, if people heard of you at all, it was for your involvement in wilderness adventures. Like that rafting competition in Nepal –"

"That was three years ago. Another lifetime now."

"I read it on the wire services. I was a nature reporter for a newspaper at the time." She picked up one of the oysters and slurped it down.

"Anyway, I expected someone who does stuff like that to be more spontaneous, more—"She caught herself, but as usual, it was too late.

"*Fun?*" Eric demanded, his rich, low voice heavy with sarcasm. The eyes had shifted back to her, burning into her with some barely contained emotion she could hardly identify. Despite the urge to lower her own gaze, she stood her ground.

"Yes. I thought you'd be more fun."

Eric's huge shoulders sagged as though someone had laid a fifty-pound weight on his back. "I suppose when one is trying to manage a business employing thousands of people, the tendency to be in control carries into all sorts of unexpected areas."

His smile hinted at melancholy, and Amanda wrestled with an urge to stroke his cheek and tell him everything would be all right. Instead, she reached for her *limoncello*, her second of the night, and took a big, calming sip. She had the feeling he was getting into a confessional mood, and she'd need the courage that comes from a bottle to take advantage of it. As a reporter, even one stripped of her recorder, she could use that mood and end the night with a juicy story after all—even without his knowledge and permission. That's what any good celebrity newshound would do. That's what Dan would do. And yet—

"My father is a control freak. Or was, before his heart condition slowed him down," Eric said. "But oh, my brother. He was the worst control freak I've ever met."

He swirled his glass of *gavi di gavi* and studied its golden cast in the fairy lights.

"What? Did he choose the underwear for his women too?"

Eric's lips turned up, and his eyes closed, like a man savoring a fine piece of music. "You do say what you think, don't you, Amanda?"

Her heart skipped at the sound of her name on his lips. She tried to diffuse the feeling with some witty comeback, but he'd begun to speak again.

"I doubt Antony picked his women's clothing for them. I don't think he made much time for women, what with running the company's day-to-day operations. I used to tease him about it, but now, I suppose I've become the same way. Lord knows, this has been my longest dry spell since the upstairs maid took an interest in me on my sixteenth birthday."

Amanda snorted a mouthful of *limoncello* up her nose and dissolved into a sputtering cough.

Eric speared a bit of lobster from one of the plates and popped it into his mouth with a mischievous smile. No, scratch mischievous. That smile was positively dirty. Amanda realized she was staring, just staring at his mouth as he chewed and swallowed the lobster meat. She shook herself back into some semblance of composure.

"What an odd thing to say," she challenged him.

"What, about the maid? I assure you it's quite true."

"No," Amanda persisted. "I mean the bit about the dry spell. How dry could a year with Stacey Dakota be?"

"You'd be surprised."

Was he trying to play Amanda again? For heaven's sake, Stacey Dakota's libido was notorious. Although perhaps not so much, now that she was allegedly on the wagon. At least that would make Eric's interest in Amanda a little less inexplicable. After all, her mother had always said, if a man doesn't get what he needs at home—.

Better not to finish that thought at all.

Amanda turned her attention to the array of dishes spread out before them. "What's this one?" She pointed her fork at some little yellow dumpling shapes.

"That, my dear, is saffron gnocchi with shaved truffles."

Amanda gaped at him, then let loose with a full, throaty laugh. "Wow, you pull out all the stops to impress a woman, don't you?"

"Only some women." He looked away again, at the tablecloth, as if he'd embarrassed himself.

Amanda pretended she hadn't heard him and concentrated her attention on the food. "That sounds decadent. I've got to have it."

The gnocchi melted in her mouth, leaving a savory tang on her tongue. Amanda gave a little shiver, her eyes flickering shut with sheer delight. The food, the starry sky above—even if she went home without a story and got fired, at least she'd always have the memory of this night and this dinner. With this man.

When she opened her eyes, Eric's gaze burned into her own, his blue the cold, deep color of the ocean that lay beyond their little haven amongst the fairy lights. He stared at her with an intensity that made her feel naked and defenseless.

Oh, he would be fierce in bed. Maybe even a little rough, domineering. It occurred to Amanda that sometimes being a control freak could be a good thing. She struggled to swallow past a lump in her throat.

Eric leaned forward and spoke, his voice low and husky with restrained desire. "I told you you're a woman of strong appetites. I intend to satisfy all of them."

Amanda's breath caught and stopped for a split second. Heat flared somewhere deep in the pit of her stomach and traveled lower still. She could almost feel his hands on her—slipping down the length of her body, sliding along her thigh, coming to rest between her legs, touching her and coaxing her warmth into a blazing fire. Silence lingered around them, growing loud in its intensity.

At last, Eric spoke again. "Taste this," he urged. He lifted a forkful of the lobster to her mouth. Its champagne sauce dripped onto the tablecloth while he awaited her decision.

Amanda barely hesitated. She opened wide for him, and then chewed the lobster with deliberate, suggestive slowness. After she swallowed, she licked her lips with great care, staring at him all the while.

"You missed a spot." Eric reached across the table. Using his thumb, he stroked away a little drip of sauce that remained on her chin. Then, he licked the sauce from his thumb, his eyes never leaving her face.

Amanda squirmed in her seat and suppressed a little moan. She'd just realized there was something else Dan might do in a situation like this one, and it had nothing to do with getting a story.

"What are you thinking?" Eric grinned.

"I'm thinking I just went off-duty for the night."

"Did you?" His blue eyes twinkled as he bent his head closer to hers again. The spicy scent of his cologne tickled her nose. "Been working too hard, have you?"

"Yes. Entirely." Her body shifted towards him of its own accord, yearning towards him.

"Not anymore, though. I'm on Capri, damn it. I'm done chasing stories about the fun other people are having. I want to have some fun of my own."

"I do hope you'll let me help you with that." Eric's satiny voice sent a slow trickle of sweat down her spine. The look on his face reminded Amanda of a cat contemplating a bowl of cream. Belatedly, she suspected she'd done a little too much blurting for one night.

~ *Four* ~

Eric Greyford didn't believe in haste, Amanda thought. They'd left *Da Paolino* a little while ago, and now they were ensconced at a table in the *Piazzetta*, eating ice cream. Maybe he'd decided she wasn't his type, and he was trying to let her down easily. She reined in her own restlessness and adopted a cheerful tone.

"Gelato was not what I expected when you offered to help me enjoy Capri."

"I try not to rush things." He dipped a spoon into the cup of melon-kiwi gelato and held it to her lips. "I didn't see any point in buying two cups of the same flavor."

"Thrift was always my mother's watchword. She'd be very impressed."

A crooked smile brightened Eric's piercing gaze. Amanda's heart skipped again as she opened her mouth to him. She'd had sex that wasn't as much fun as sharing this cup of ice cream.

She swallowed and dabbed a napkin to her lips. "I don't mind the slow and thorough approach. I'm thinking that's the difference between the guys I usually date and a billionaire playboy. Attention to details."

Amanda knew Eric's original intent in inviting her out had been nothing more than casual sex. Yet, even after she'd made the remark about looking for fun, he'd remained the perfect gentleman, attentive and patient. After the meal, he'd taken her back to the *gelateria*, and when he discovered she'd hardly seen any of the island's famous tourist attractions, he'd suggested they go sightseeing together. Maybe he was afraid Stacey would find them if he took Amanda back to his hotel. The mysterious arrangement with Stacey weighed on Amanda's mind, though not nearly as much as it would have if that mind had been free of *limoncello*. Amanda wasn't the sort to poach another girl's boyfriend. But maybe the arrangement involved both Eric and Stacey having their little flings. Her time as a reporter at *Fame* had made it clear that celebrities played by a whole different set of rules than ordinary people in places like Lake Havasu.

Yes, if Amanda was sure she wanted a quick, meaningless fling, then Eric would be the ideal man for the job. All she had to do was ask him back to her room. She studied him as he sat across from her, swept away again by his high cheekbones, beautifully defined lips, and his dark wavy hair, which just brushed the collar of his crisp linen shirt. The very idea of inviting this man back to her hotel made her palms go all sweaty. She should get out before she did something insane. She had a better sense of him now, and he wasn't quite as threatening as he'd appeared at their first meeting. If she called a halt to this little game they were playing, he'd accept it and send her on her way. But did she want to call a halt?

Amanda didn't do casual, not ever. She'd spent her life watching her mother pine for a guy that was supposed to have been a casual affair. Despite being a single parent, her mom had plenty of suitors. However, she'd rejected every one of them, preferring a life alone and a scrapbook of memories of her romance with the pre-billionaire Peter Tate.

But Amanda was older, probably a lot more experienced than her mom had been in a similar situation. And her mother and Peter Tate had had a genuine affair, one that had lasted well over a year, judging from her mother's stories. Amanda was under no delusions that Eric Greyford offered her anything similar. She'd tried to learn from her mother's mistake, pursuing only serious, long-term relationships. All three of them had ended badly, with Amanda thrown over for someone else—someone usually described as more "fun." Even before arriving in Capri, she'd begun to think she needed to go to the other extreme—abandon all hope of emotional fulfillment with a guy and embrace the superficial. Now, she needed only Eric's cooperation in the matter—before she completely lost her nerve.

"I'm ready to see those sights," she said, as Eric offered her the last spoonful of gelato.

"Are you now?"

His cocky smile rattled Amanda's new resolve—but only a little.

Eric wanted to believe she was ready to satisfy his long ignored urges. But would she also be ready to move on when he was through with her? For Eric and the women he usually dated, sex was more of a sport than an emotional commitment. He doubted that was how Amanda saw things, despite her determined effort at flirtation. If anything, she was being a little too determined. Again the thought that she might be a corporate spy for Tate Global crossed his mind.

Ahead of him, she sashayed through the *Piazzetta* with a slightly drunken grace. How she could move so effortlessly in the cobbled square on those heels was a source of endless fascination to Eric. She seemed to bring out the gawking teenager in him, much to his consternation. He'd barely been able to control himself while sitting beside her in the restaurant, and even now, if he touched her bare arm, he feared he'd erupt like Vesuvius. He should have made more time for mindless anonymous sex in the last few months—penciled it right in the book, in between board meetings and festival preparations and speeches to restive stockholders. He could imagine Cathy's solemn expression never changing, even as she jotted "Sex at six" into his daily planner.

He shook himself out of his reverie and took several gulps of the crisp salt air, clearing his mind.

Amanda stopped moving. Moonlight shone in her hair as she tossed him a backward glance. "Which way from here?" she asked. "And shouldn't I be following you? You know your way around this island better than I do."

She planted her hands on her hips—full, round, welcoming hips and petite hands with no rings. Her nails were short and unpainted, even a little ragged—the hands of a woman who did something with her day, rather than spending it lounging beside a pool and complaining about the quality of her maid service. Cathy said she'd been a nature reporter, and her tanned body reflected the time she must have spent outdoors. The golden tones of her skin were authentic, not something that washed off in the shower. A natural girl with no jewelry and no perfume except the one she'd bought this morning—the very image dazzled him, so contrary was it to the women he'd had in the past.

He strolled up to her side and spoke. "I say, didn't you mention you were an environmental reporter once? I'm thinking of greatly expanding Greyford's environmental coverage. Possibly even starting up some new publications in that field. What do you think of the idea?"

"I think I'd like to apply for a job, sir." Amanda laughed, and the merry openhearted sound went straight to his heart.

"I'd be happy to have you."

"Does Stacey like the great outdoors, too?" Amanda asked.

The answer to that was an emphatic no. He'd talked Stacey into a camping trip a number of months ago. Two days into the adventure, she'd fled to the nearest luxury hotel.

"It's not one of her favorite things."

Amanda grinned. "I went camping and canoeing a lot back in Arizona—but that's pretty tame stuff. I've always wanted to do whitewater rafting—and all those other crazy sports you do."

"Are you very athletic?"

Amanda shrugged. "I'd like to say yes, because I know it would impress you. But no. I'm certainly not in your class, at any rate. I was on the rowing team in college, and I did okay, probably because I got to sit in one spot the whole time. Also, it wasn't a very good team. With most team sports, it's much safer for all concerned if I stay on the sidelines and watch. I once gave a friend a concussion when we were playing volleyball."

Eric laughed.

"So I like the outdoors, but I wouldn't call myself a real athlete. But I admire athletes, especially people like you who can do all that risky stuff like snowmobiling and whitewater rafting. And you race cars, too, don't you? Dan— that's my editor—she mentioned you did. That must be quite a thrill."

"No, not anymore. Not since –"

The darkness rose up in him again, the same darkness that had been threatening to engulf him for a year now. The warm, sensuous mood between them evaporated more quickly than a rain cloud in the Capri sky. He cursed under his breath and clenched his fists.

"I'm so sorry!" Amanda covered her mouth with her hand. "Your brother. The car crash. That was incredibly insensitive of me."

Eric thrust his hands into the pockets of his trousers. "It's fine. I'm fine."

"But you aren't," Amanda insisted, her eyes searching every inch of his face. "Were you two very close?"

"As close as two brothers might be who are nearly ten years apart. Which is to say, I looked up to him, and he put up with me. I'd rather not talk about him." He fixed her with a stern warning look, but like most reporters, she failed to take the hint.

"Sometimes talking about things helps."

She reached towards him, then seemed to think better of the gesture and withdrew. Eric hated the disappointment that coursed through his veins, the weakness of it. She was meant to be an empty diversion for an evening, and instead, she fancied herself a psychotherapist. He should have had her arrested after all, and then made a date with that empty-headed Italian model, the one who didn't speak English. Hell, she barely spoke Italian.

"Is that the road?" Amanda asked, frantically trying to make amends for her *faux pas*. She gestured beyond the town hall to a narrow stony lane.

"Yes, it is."

She peered down the narrow path and hesitated. "And that's really the way to the fantastic view?"

Behind her, Eric watched as a light breeze ruffled the loose wisps of her wheat-gold hair. She looked askance at him again, with a timid, girlish smile.

"Yes," he admitted. "The view is quite fantastic."

Moving ahead of her in the crowd, he stretched out a hand and then pulled it back, stuffing it into his pocket once again. He'd nearly taken her hand. Wouldn't that look grand in all the tabloids, what with everyone thinking he was Stacey's boyfriend? More than her boyfriend, judging by the photographer's 'Mr. Stacey Dakota' remark earlier in the day.

Eric wondered if Stacey was looking forward to their publicly staged break-up after the festival as much as he was. Although he didn't regret the friendship that had grown out of their proximity, Eric seriously regretted allowing the public to believe the two of them were lovers. He'd exploded in fury when he'd realized his own brother had planted the initial rumors about his "love affair" with Stacey, a mercenary effort to boost Greyford Publishing's name recognition and give it a more youthful image. His last conversation with his brother had been an argument about the stories.

"Hello in there!" Amanda's sing-song voice intruded on his thoughts.

"Sorry. Thinking about work."

"I must be pretty disappointing company, then, if I can't keep a man's mind off a pile of newspapers for a few hours."

Eric halted in front of the *Piazzetta*'s famous clock tower. "No, you aren't disappointing me at all. I have a great deal on my mind. I'm sorry if I'm being inattentive."

"Hey, I told you I'd give up on the story for *Fame.*" Amanda grinned, her chocolaty brown eyes sparkling at him. "I'm here because you promised to show me the sights, but if you're not in the mood, I can go back to my room."

"Don't." He closed the distance between them. He wanted to crush her against his chest right here, right now. Forget the crowds and the public image, forget everything else as he learned the taste of her skin and the sounds she would make as he touched her in her most secret places. "I don't want you to go. Not yet. Let's enjoy the night—with no hidden agenda on either of our parts. You say you've abandoned your story. I'll abandon my rather base designs on you, and we'll just—"

"What? Be friends?" Amanda gave a sharp laugh, eying him as though she feared he might become dangerous at any moment.

Eric's skill with women, once legendary among his friends, had vanished under Amanda's unnerving combination of naïve goodwill and cynical humor. While he struggled for a witty comeback, she turned away from him. With a twitch of her hips, she was strolling ahead, up the narrow medieval road that led to the *Arco Naturale.*

Eric lagged behind, preferring to watch the high, round shape of her luscious bottom as she climbed the road's slight incline. That bottom could make a man commit treason. The constricted sensation in his groin began to flare again, and he cursed himself for trying to play the bloody gentleman with her. Her curvaceous body cried out for the very opposite of gentlemanly behavior.

"I have to admit," Amanda called over her shoulder, "this isn't what I expected you to suggest when I said I was looking for fun."

"And what were you expecting?"

"I don't know—a quick hustle back to your room and a tumble in the sheets before being kicked into the hallway around two a.m."

Eric eyed her back with unabashed amusement. Her bluntness reminded him of Stacey, but he liked Amanda's packaging much better. He hastened to join her. "You Americans do say what you think."

"Well, isn't it what you were planning?"

That had been his intention when he'd first found her in his room, bent over that dresser drawer in her tight skirt and sky-high heels. The idea still held its attraction. Yet he couldn't believe that was what Amanda wanted.

They rounded a corner on the twisting, ancient road. Stone houses lined either side of the street, crowding so near they gave one a sensation of claustrophobia. The noise from the *Piazzetta* faded away, like music on a radio when the batteries have run down. Few people passed them, and those who did looked more like island natives than upscale tourists. Amanda began to understand Eric wasn't moving so slowly after all. He was merely drawing her away from the bustling crowds down at the center of Capri, leading her to some lonely, wild place where he didn't have to worry about the prying eyes of hotel clerks or paparazzi. Now would be the time to bail out, if ever.

"So you wrote for newspapers before you went over to the dark side and joined Tate Global Multimedia?" Eric asked, his brandy-smooth voice rendering her defenseless and sparking an electric jolt in her belly.

"Um, yes." She glanced at him, and then turned her attention to a less exciting sight, an old house that sported boxes of trailing bougainvillea at every window. "It's so beautiful here."

"Yes, it is."

Amanda dared not look back at Eric when he spoke. She could tell from the husky timbre of his voice that he wasn't referring to the flowers.

"Talk to me," he urged. "How'd you wind up working for *Fame*?"

"My mother encouraged me to take the job before she passed away. The pay is phenomenal compared to what I made at the Lake Havasu Star."

"I'm sure it is," he purred, his soothing voice hypnotic in this quiet place.

"Deep down I kept hoping –"

"What did you hope?"

There, she'd almost gone and told him about her childish dreams of forging a real relationship with Peter Tate. She didn't want anyone to know that man was her father, least of all Eric Greyford. Tate Global was trying to take over his family-run company, after all. He'd never speak to her again if he learned who her father was. The fact that she should care about any future conversations with Eric proved clearly that she'd had too much to drink at the restaurant. This is all about the now, she reminded herself. No worries about future conversations.

"Amanda? What did you hope?"

"Nothing much," she shrugged. "I guess I hoped I'd learn to like it. But I don't. In fact, I may not be doing it much longer. I may resign when I go back to New York."

Where the heck had that come from?

Eric stopped walking and turned to face her.

"You could work for me. I was serious earlier. We aren't like Tate Global. Our papers and magazines focus on hard news. Or they did, until my brother started trying to compete head-on with Tate. I think that was a mistake, rather like a mouse roaring at a lion—all he did was cause Tate to pay even more attention to us."

Eric reached up and ruffled his unruly hair in a gesture of exasperation.

Amanda longed to run her own fingers through those thick, dark waves. Would his chest be full of dark hair too, or bare and smooth? Somewhere in the files of Fame there must be pictures of him shirtless. How could she have missed those? Maybe pictures of him at the beach with Stacey, or images from some of his high profile outdoor activities—yachting, diving, climbing. Okay, definitely no shirtless pictures of him climbing mountains, that would be weird. Yet there must be more pictures somewhere. Of course, she could just let the night play out as he'd originally envisioned it. She'd get to find out for herself first hand. Meanwhile, she'd have to focus her energy on maintaining some semblance of conversational skills.

"I appreciate the offer," she told Eric as they resumed their walk. "But I don't know what I want to do next. Maybe go back to the newspaper where I used to work in Arizona. They'd be happy to have me. Or I was thinking about getting into teaching. I like kids, and it looks like it's going to be quite a while before I have any of my own. And with a job like that, I'd have more time to have a personal life, you know?"

Eric chuckled. "I used to have one of those. Now, I meet."

"You meet?"

"Board meetings, meetings with advertisers, stockholder meetings. I meet. That's what I spend my life doing now."

"Couldn't someone else do the day-to-day running things and you just sit on the board and, I don't know, collect cash from your stock options?"

Eric narrowed his eyes and gave her a sharp, suspicious gaze. She'd meant to offer friendly concern, but he was clearly wondering if the reporter in her was gathering intel for a story. Come to think of it, maybe she *was* gathering intel for a story. Dan would be the first to tell her she could have her cake and eat it too. So to speak. Have fun, but not too much fun. Keep it casual, get a good story, get the guy—and then get the heck out of town. That's what Dan would do. Eric's creamy English accent totally disrupted Amanda's line of reasoning.

"My father very much wants me to be the one running the company," he said. "He wants it to remain under family control. In fact, though, the family control is an illusion. The stockholders and the board are what control a public corporation. I'm a rubber stamp for their recommendations. I've been trying to find a way to change that, but so far, I haven't found a good one. Unlike your employer, Greyford Publishing is a very conservative company, very old line. It took some effort for my father to convince them to appoint me as acting Chief Operating Officer after Antony died. Some days, I'm sorry he succeeded."

Amanda frowned. Although the alcohol at dinner had loosened her up, made her feel more willing to be spontaneous and experimental, it appeared to be having the opposite effect on Eric.

"Are you sorry you inherited your brother's job?" she asked.

"I suppose I am."

She got the feeling he was trying the words on for size, discovering the truth of them for the first time.

"I couldn't say no," he added after a long pause. "I had other plans, but my father's health is failing. He made it clear he needed me. Fathers can be like that."

A stab of jealousy knifed Amanda's heart. "I wouldn't know. Mine was never around."

They stopped at the crest of a steep hill, beside a small whitewashed medieval church. Only a few inches separated them, and Eric turned to face her, the spicy scent of him addling her concentration once more. His gaze locked with hers and concern creased his smooth brow. "Is your father dead?"

"No, just couldn't be bothered." Trying for a levity she didn't feel, Amanda added, "I'm his shameful secret. My parents weren't married."

"Ah." Eric nodded, his eyes searching her face, apparently trying to gauge how to respond to her news.

"It's no big deal."

"But rough luck for you." His voice was soft. A look of tender sympathy darkened his eyes, and he raised a hand to her face. With the care of an artist, he used his fingertips to trace the lines of her cheekbones. "If your mother was half the beauty you are, a man would have to be insane to abandon her."

"Oh." Amanda lost all command of the English language as his touch went on, exploring the shape of her nose, her cheeks, her throat. At last, his fingers came to rest, cupping her chin in his hand like a snifter of brandy.

"Enough about business. I'm thinking about kissing you right now." A wry smile turned up one corner of his mouth.

Amanda smiled and relaxed into his touch. "I'm thinking about it too."

His lips brushed against hers, tentative and gentle, then more firmly. His tongue parted her lips, invading her with a restrained force that both excited and alarmed her. He backed her up against the church wall, his hands slipping down along the sides of her body, tracing her contours with sensuous attention. When he broke the kiss at last, his fingers laced through hers and clasped her hand tight.

"Shall we go on?" His voice flowed over her like the sweetest honey.

"Yes." She nodded. "I'd like that."

He led her up over the crest of the hill. Beyond the edges of the old medieval city, they entered onto a much wilder path, lined with scrubby pine trees and sturdy, long-stemmed wildflowers. The full moon cast its silvery glow on everything around them. Beneath one of the taller pine trees, he stopped. Some distance ahead, Amanda glimpsed the sea. A shaft of light split the dark, still waters and seemed to point its way towards them. All around, she heard the cries of night birds and the flutter of their wings.

"It's very peaceful here." She looked up at him, but his face lay in deep shadow. She didn't want to feel uneasy, and yet she did. Not that she thought Eric was in some way a danger to her. Her own feelings were the real problem. She wanted to be wild and sexy and adventurous, the way Dan would be in this situation. Yet she also couldn't help wondering—what would happen afterward? If this evening was a slow build-up to getting her into bed, would she find herself out in that hotel corridor the next morning? And would she be able to deal with that?

Eric tugged on her hand to get her attention. "Your thoughts are a million miles away."

"No, I'm thinking very much about what's happening right now." She disengaged her hand from his and went to lean against the pine tree. "Do you think you might want to kiss me again?" she asked, in the most seductive voice she could manage. Her blood pounded in her ears, and she was glad of the darkness, knowing that her face must have turned scarlet when she spoke so boldly.

With silent, feline grace, Eric stalked towards her. He braced a hand above her, against the craggy bark of the tree. He stroked a thumb down the side of her face, stopping to trace the outline of her lips, and she opened them for him without even thinking about it. His thumb darted into her mouth, and she nibbled at it playfully.

Eric's nostrils flared as he caught his breath. He leaned his head down to her. His lips smothered hers, urgent and demanding, unrelenting. Amanda arched towards him, feeling the heat of him all up and down her body. His hands came down around her waist and held her tight against the hard evidence of his own arousal as the kiss continued. He tasted of the *limoncello* and the wine they'd had earlier, and Amanda thought she would be drunk with the taste of him.

Eric's lips moved away from hers as he nuzzled her, nibbling at the side of her neck. His hand skimmed over her hip and down her thigh. He caught the hem of her skirt and slipped his hand under it. She should stop him, really she should. This was crazy and irresponsible and self-indulgent. But she'd made the choice for crazy when she followed him to this lonely place. It was probably too late to back out now.

His fingers stroked her bare thigh beneath the skirt. Amanda sighed. With his other hand, he turned her face up to his and crushed his lips against hers. His hand slithered between her legs in an intimate caress, and she was ready for him. So ready it was embarrassing. He rained a flurry of kisses down on her hair, her face, and her throat, as he continued to toy with her. Her legs wobbled in the three-inch heels, and she nearly collapsed, shaky with excitement and fear.

"I haven't wanted anyone this much in a very long time." Eric's low whisper sent a shiver through her. His hand slipped from between her legs, and he moved to lower her to the ground.

They were so close now, so close. Their haste and urgency was unlike anything Amanda had ever experienced. The way he'd crushed her to him, the fire in his eyes when he looked at her—the intensity of his desire for her amazed her. She'd thought she wanted casual sex, but could anything that passed between them be casual? It felt like quite the opposite—like something earth-shattering that threatened to break into her life and disrupt every little piece of it. And it would, she realized with a start. Come the morning, everything about her would be different if she went through with this.

"Wait, wait." She hated herself even as she spoke. Pressing a hand against his chest, she pushed, gently but firmly. "I'm sorry, Eric. I just can't do this."

~ *Five* ~

Eric saw her face change in an instant, saw her trying to fight her own inhibitions. She bit her lower lip, and her breath caught on a sigh as she shivered against him. When she spoke up, it came as no surprise. Indeed, in a strange way, he found himself relieved. More times than he could count, he'd played this game and won. Flirt with a shallow, empty-headed girl, spirit her off to some out-of-the-way spot and give her a quick tumble, then forget her the next day. Pure, meaningless sex. That's what he'd been looking for tonight, but that wasn't what he'd get with a girl like Amanda. Even with all the blood still rushing away from his brain and heading to points south, he understood there would be nothing meaningless, nothing at all shallow, about sex between the two of them.

Regarding her in the moonlight, he saw that her elegant updo was gone, her hair a tousled, sexy mess that made him want her all over again. She laid a hand on his arm.

"I don't think you should touch me right now." He swallowed hard. "The bad news hasn't made it to every part of my body yet."

She drew back her hand like she'd been burned. "I'm sorry. I don't mean to be a tease."

Eric straightened. Forgetting the warning he'd given her, he laid his hand on her cheek. "Don't think that of yourself. It's always a woman's right to change her mind. Even in this age of birth control, you still have far more at stake than I do. I suppose you know that better than most people, because of your parents."

She stared down at the ground, as though he was scolding her, and he cursed himself for embarrassing her. Although why that should matter to him, he couldn't say. He did have every right to be furious, or at least damned aggravated with her. Yet instead, a ridiculous tenderness came over him whenever he looked at her. "Look here," he said. "You tried something new. It wasn't to your liking. Rather how I felt when I tried sushi."

Amanda managed a weak laugh.

"There may have been a time when I'd have been annoyed with you, but this has been an educational year for me in all regards. This is probably for the best. Stacey says there are three kinds of women, you know."

Amanda eyes narrowed. "She says that, does she?"

"Those who do, those who don't—and those who do but then regret it horribly next morning. You would have been in the last category. I've suspected it all night, but I got a bit carried away by the sight of you in that dress."

"I suppose I should thank Stacey for helping you to understand women so well."

Eric paced away from her and took several quick, deep breaths. No luck. Parts of him were still stiff with shock, so to speak. Amanda stepped away from the tree she'd been leaning against, brushing off her dress.

How had he dared?

The half-formed thought startled him when it popped into his head, but he knew it for truth. She was engrossed in picking pine needles out of her moonlit hair, barely aware of him beside her. Every move she made was so simple and fluid, it brought a lump to his throat. He should have done better by her, should have spent weeks wining and dining her. And when he bedded her, it should have been in a real bed, with rose-scented sheets and buckets of champagne to toast her magnificent eyes.

"I guess we should head back." Amanda eyed him with a look of patient concern.

How long had he been staring at her? The blood must not have found its way back to his brain yet. What he needed was a bracing shower. Possibly even two. Yet he didn't want to say good-bye to her, which made no sense. Good Lord, if he didn't get himself under control as soon as possible, he'd be sending her flowers or doing something even more overwrought—writing love poetry.

Amanda gave him a timid wave and backed away, heading down the slope they'd climbed.

"Hang on!" he called, following her. He caught her elbow, then snatched his hand back when she stared at it in amazement. "I promised I'd show you the Arch. Why don't we do that? We're almost there."

Amanda eyed him with comical skepticism.

He raised his hands like a man surrendering, then stuffed them in his pockets. "Just as a friend. I hate for us to part like this. My word of honor, I'm not trying anything with you again."

She blinked a few times but said nothing.

"I won't try anything tonight, at any rate. I don't know if my body could handle another round. But a walk might do me good."

When she nodded her agreement, he was thrilled and disgusted, marveling that he, Eric Greyford, had practically begged a woman to stay with him. He should definitely call that supermodel tomorrow. She'd be able to put out this fire.

They walked beside one another, both silent and preoccupied. After a short stroll through the narrow thicket of pine trees, they came into a wide clearing on a high plateau. To Amanda, the Natural Arch looked like the remnant of some ancient portal to a fairy castle.

"What is it? Or what did it used to be?" she asked.

"It used to be a grotto." The rich depth of Eric's baritone gave her a chill and made her knees shake. Even when he'd started talking about Stacey Dakota, his voice had turned her on. Lucky Stacey, to hear that voice every day, possibly for the rest of her life.

"The elements eroded the stone," Eric continued. "And now all that's left is the arch. A doorway to nothing."

Amanda stepped into the archway. "Doesn't it look like you could walk through it and disappear into another universe?"

Eric's back stiffened, and he reached a hand out to her. She backed up another step, afraid to have all those urges come rushing at her again. She wouldn't be able to refuse him a second time.

He drew his hand back. "You might not disappear into another universe, but you could go right over the edge of the cliff."

Amanda turned and looked off to the side. About a half-meter in front of her, the uneven terrain came to an abrupt stop. She turned fully and looked out over the Tyrrhenian Sea. Moonglow shone down on the water, and the dark outline of the Italian mainland loomed in the distance. She'd always been comfortable in high places, the schoolgirl who frightened her friends by getting too close to the edge on their annual field trips to the Grand Canyon. Now she stepped a few inches closer to the land's end, wanting to look over at the rocky outcroppings below. Like lightning, Eric was upon her, yanking her back through the archway and pulling her against him.

"What are you doing?" he demanded.

"I just wanted to look down at the water!" Amanda's voice shook. Anger warred with excitement at being in his arms again. There'd still been a good foot of ground between her and the edge, so he couldn't truly believe she was in real danger. It had to be another attempt to get close to her, so he could add another name to his list of conquests.

She squirmed in his arms and was taken aback at what she saw when she turned to face him. His eyes were wide and wild with—fear?

"Were you afraid?"

His eyes narrowed to stern, angry slits, and he released her in silence.

She stepped away from the Arch and moved in the direction of the path, not wanting to panic him again.

"I wasn't thinking," she said gently. "Your brother died so suddenly, it must make you fearful about so many things now."

"My brother has nothing to do with this. It's dark, it's late, and you've had a great deal to drink. And you're wearing those maddening shoes. You could catch a heel on a rock and lose your balance."

A great deal to drink? The nerve of him.

"Well, I didn't. Because I have a good sense of balance, and I always have, Eric. People who don't would never get that close to the edge in the first place. I think you were afraid I'd kill myself because you think everybody's going to die too soon, yourself included. Am I right?"

"I don't know what you're talking about." Clenching and unclenching his fists, Eric circled her like a hungry panther.

Amanda could have done some pacing and circling of her own right about now. Her insides were still a roiling mass of sexual frustration and anger and utter confusion. Plus, Eric's mention of Stacey had left her seething inside.

"You were known for being an outdoorsy adventurer before you took charge of your dad's company. I wouldn't expect you to balk at someone standing near the edge of a hill. Either you're trying to put the make on me again, or there's something deeper upsetting you. Or does Stacey like it when you play these mind games with her? Because I don't."

Eric whirled at her, his eyes flashing silver in the moonlight. "First of all, I don't see how Stacey comes into this discussion, or my brother. You bloody Yanks are all such a bunch of amateur psychoanalysts. Second, that is much more than a hill and you know it. And third, the key words are, 'before I took charge.' My father and brother taught me that running a business takes control and caution, not going off on crazy impulses. But I suppose crazy impulses are your trademark, what with your unique mode of introducing yourself to me and your recent performance over there in the pine trees."

That was unfair. She'd struggled to make that decision, and he'd seemed so kind and understanding in the wake of it.

"No wonder your company is so threatened, Eric," she sniped.

"I beg your pardon?" His hands curled into fists again.

"Honestly, Eric, Tate Global didn't become this great big behemoth because my fa—. It didn't become so huge because my boss was exceedingly cautious. He took risks, with the business and with people. If anybody or anything held him back, he just kicked it over the side of the boat! He's not a cautious man by nature, and I don't think you are either. But trying to become one appears to be making you miserable. I'm going back to my hotel now."

Eric glared at her with wide-eyed amazement. Amanda doubted Stacey or anyone in his stable of beauties spoke to him in this way. Well, Stacey Dakota was welcome to this temperamental snob. Amanda stalked away from him, then halted at the path into the pine trees.

"Hey," she called. "It's not like you're cautious with women, though, is it? Takes a pretty bold guy to ask someone for a date when he catches her breaking into his room. Maybe you should try treating your business the way you treat women—take what you can get from it and then toss it aside for a new one."

She turned and continued on her way. Behind her, a swift rustling sound told her that Eric had followed. He caught her by the arm and spun her to face him. "It's not my business making me crazy, woman. It's you."

His mouth came down on hers, claiming her with hungry authority. His tongue forced its way between her lips, but she took him into her willingly. Oh, the taste and smell of him again. It broke her heart. He could be so handsome and gentle and funny, and yet he was such a manipulative egotist. To have him so close and know she meant nothing to him at all, just another quickie in the woods to boast about with his rich playboy buddies. And after he'd told her he was relieved by her rejection! He only kissed her now because he was a control freak who couldn't take no for an answer.

She'd resolutely kept her hands at her sides throughout the kiss, but now she raised them, torn between pulling him closer and shoving him away.

Instead, he released her first. "Bloody hell. I don't know what came over me." He ran his hands through his hair and backed away. "I don't force myself on women. You should go."

He turned his back on her and strode towards the cliff's edge, head down and hands jammed into his pockets.

Amanda tossed and turned on her bed at the Loreley. So much for getting the big story. Not to mention missing out on an evening of uninhibited passion. She grimaced at the ceiling. Only one thing would've led to a good night's sleep for her, and she'd rejected that offer not once, but twice. No doubt, he and Stacey were together right now. A vivid image of the two of them twined together sent her pulse and temperature skyrocketing. She leapt up and boosted the room's air-conditioning another notch. She'd been doing that all night, as if cool air would ease the oppressive heat burning deep in her belly.

Going back over to the bed, Amanda picked up the tableside clock. It read two a.m., which meant it was about eight back in New York. Dan might be in her office, since she put in a lot of late hours. Amanda decided there was no time like the present to burn all her bridges, so she picked up her cell phone and dialed.

"Hey, sweetie!" Dan's gravelly voice burst through the phone's tiny speaker.

"Dan, I can't do this anymore," Amanda declared. "I want to resign."

"Now, sweetie. Did Greyford back out of the interview?"

"You could say that."

"And another prince turns out to be a frog." Dan made a dismissive razzing sound with her lips.

"Aren't they all?" Amanda flopped back down onto the bed.

"Pretty much. Sounds like you're learning."

"The hard way." Boy, had it been the hard way.

"I didn't hold out much hope, sweetie. He's the competition, after all. So what are you saying about quitting?"

Amanda took a deep breath and launched into her answer. She had no affinity for celebrity news, she was a waste of office space at Fame, and it would be for the good of all concerned.

"And what are you going to do next, eh?"

Amanda mumbled out the same reply she'd given Eric about teaching or going back to the *Lake Havasu Star.*

"That old rag?" Dan barked at her. "Sweetie, your dad will be disappointed. He wants to know that you're a go-getter. Small town newspapers are a dying breed, and I doubt he'd be willing to move you to one of his other magazines if you don't try harder here. You know him, family ties mean nothing if you don't pull your weight."

"You know, that's just it, Dan -- I don't know him. I thought I might get to know him if I took a job with one of his magazines in New York, but it hasn't worked out that way. Either he's out of town when I'm there, or I'm out of town on assignment when he's there. And I don't think that's a coincidence."

Amanda sat up again and gazed out her window at the nearby lights from the hotel's terrace bar. Dan's cheerful, tobacco-roughened voice had sparked a wave of homesickness. Home would always be Arizona, but right now, even New York seemed more welcoming than Capri.

"I want to be done and come home."

A sour note came into Dan's voice. "You can't come home. You are on this staff, and you'll stay on it until I receive a written resignation. And if you know what's good for you, you'll give at least two weeks notice. Writing for *Fame* is a dream job for a lot of young reporters, ones who aren't related to the publisher."

Amanda bristled. "I never asked for special treatment!"

"No, that's true." Dan's tone softened. "Let me put it this way, Amanda. Whether or not you like the job is immaterial right now. You need to act like a professional, and your daddy issues are keeping you from doing that. Now, you're in Capri on this magazine's dime, and you will have to stay there until this festival is over. I have a lot of events going on, and the staff is spread pretty thin. I'm not bringing you home until Stacey Dakota closes down the show in a week and a half. Concentrate on doing some behind the scenes interviews with people and little news briefs on which celebs have arrived, who they're dating, what they're wearing. You can do that much."

"Yeah, I can."

"Of course you can," Dan insisted, clucking like a mother hen. "I'm telling you, sweetie. Your real problem is you need to find yourself a pool boy or a handsome waiter. Your hormones are taking over your bloodstream. You need to get them back in balance."

Amanda laughed at the cynical older woman's advice. "I gave it my best shot earlier today, Dan. I'm not cut out for the quickie mentality. It's a little too squalid for me."

Dan gave an exaggerated harrumph. "Squalid, is it? Hey, sweetie, one person's squalid is another person's way of life. Mine, to be exact."

"Sorry."

Amanda got up off the bed and stalked out to her little second-floor balcony, drinking in the gentle Mediterranean breeze that swirled around her. The night was warm but not too hot and humid. There was no real need for the air conditioning at all, other than her own irritable wish to shut out happy sounds from the revelers at the café across the street.

Dan spoke up again. "Hey, you know what you can do for me? This is big."

The last thing Amanda wanted to deal with now was a "big" story. No doubt, it would involve someone famous getting falling down drunk.

"What is it?"

"This might be up your alley. There's a pre-festival event day after tomorrow—a big, sophisticated fundraiser party at Franco Battali's villa. It's his land they're using for the concerts this weekend. Anyway, the party is a fundraiser for some wilderness conservation charity that Eric Greyford set up a few years ago."

"Really?" Amanda's interest was piqued in spite of herself.

"Yeah, you know him with all that outdoors stuff."

"So what exactly do you want?" Amanda asked. "Specific interviews? Or a general rundown about the event?"

"General stuff," Dan agreed. "Some brief blurbs about who's there and what's up with them. You up for it?"

"Sure," Amanda sighed.

"I was going to send Zeke alone, but it'll be better with you there to add some detail."

Inwardly, Amanda groaned at the thought of dragging Zeke along with her to a party at an Italian villa. The man dressed like a thrift store had blown up in his face.

Dan read her thoughts. "Try to get Zeke to wear a suit. I know he has one. Tell him this Battali guy is very stylish and will have him thrown out on his ear if he shows up in jeans."

"I'll tell him," Amanda agreed. "I can't make him do it, though."

"No, I suppose not," Dan admitted. "Now, listen, as for your own concerns - when the festival is over, if you still want to resign, we'll talk."

"I will."

"Then you'll do it the right way. You'll put it in writing. You'll give at least two weeks notice. And you'll break the news to your dad, not me."

As if her father would care that she wanted to resign. Well, he might, at that. He didn't like anyone who failed to adequately worship him. Amanda slumped into a wrought iron chair on the balcony and sighed. "Agreed. I'll tell him."

"Great, sweetie. Now go find yourself a pool boy."

"I don't want one. I hate all men."

"Me too, honey. But they are handy for opening jars—and for that other thing."

Amanda gave a short laugh.

"Listen!" Dan exclaimed. "While I have you on the phone, here's one other thing to keep an eye out for while you're in Capri."

"What's that?"

"We got an anonymous tip that Stacey's parents are coming to Capri to see her show. And when I say anonymous, I mean that Stacey's mother called me up and told me herself, off the record, of course."

"Of course. And that's a big deal because?"

"Listen, you think you have Daddy issues?" Dan drew Amanda in with her homey, gossipy tone. "Stacey's parents are terrors. All they care about is how much cash the kid rakes in and how much of it they can get for themselves. Legally, she's an adult now, but they're still her business managers. Anyway, whenever they show up, she goes off the rails. This could mean lots of drunk, angry Stacey stories, and the public hasn't seen any of those in over a year. They're chomping at the bit for a good celebrity meltdown."

Amanda should despise Stacey Dakota. Clearly, Eric cared for her more than he let on. Her mind drifted back to the moment he'd told her he was relieved to be refused. And then he'd started babbling about Stacey. However, while Amanda had plenty of reason to be jealous, she couldn't look forward to the girl having a public meltdown. She understood all too well the desperate need to please a parent who never seemed satisfied. Amanda suspected she and Stacey both might be better off cutting their parents out of their lives, but it was hard to give up on the dream of a perfect family.

"I'm thinking once Stacey and the 'rents get together, it's going to be like watching a million dollar soap opera, only live and with real people," Dan boasted.

Amanda's conscience twinged her again. If she stayed at *Fame* much longer, she'd have to get the thing surgically removed. Stacey had become notorious for not showing up at rehearsals or arriving in a state of sloppy inebriation. She'd been photographed passed out in more bars than Amanda had ever visited. But all of that was a long time ago in Hollywood years.

Despite her dad's fondness for negative stories about Stacey in *Fame* and his other publications, Amanda knew the singer was as popular as ever. Her new CD was climbing the charts, and she seemed to be putting on a newer, happier face. Her relationship with Eric must be the reason. At any rate, it pained Amanda to think of people like Dan rooting for a big public blow-up between Stacey and her controlling parents.

"Are you asking me to interview the parents?" She could hardly keep the disgust from her voice.

"You won't even have to do that. Just hang around and watch the sparks fly. And rumor has it—and by that I mean, Stacey's mom says—they're bringing Artemisia Nash with them."

"Who?"

"Wedding planner to the stars, sweetie. Now that could be a fun interview. You can talk to Artemisia about some of the great weddings she's planned and how she pulls it all together. Try to scope out what she has in mind for Stacey and Eric. Boy, that marriage won't last a year, if I'm any expert. And believe me, I am. That London lothario couldn't be faithful to one woman for five minutes. Didn't he make a pass at you last night?"

"No. Nothing like that. You must have misunderstood."

"Oh. Too bad. See if you can schedule a meet with Artemisia, 'kay?"

"Sure thing. Text me her contact info." Amanda made some excuses and got off the phone as quick as she could. She let out a frustrated scream, then marched into her room and threw the phone down on the bed. It landed with a mild, unsatisfying whoosh that did nothing at all to placate her anger.

~ *Six* ~

Eric lay on a chaise lounge at the *Bagni da Maria* within sight of where his friend Franco had docked his yacht for the day. Although much of Capri's rocky shores proved inhospitable for sunbathing, in certain wide, level areas, private beach clubs had grown up over the years. Eric had always been willing to pay for the right to be left alone, but never more so than today.

Unfortunately, he doubted this area was sufficiently private. A few meters east, colorful bathing huts lined the portion of the beach open to the general public, and above Eric, on a high ledge, sat the club's outdoor restaurant. Its location would afford any voyeur with the right tools an excellent glimpse into what went on down here amongst the beautiful people. No doubt, the paparazzi were readying their telephoto lenses, even as Eric tried to forget their existence—and the fact that he himself employed a ridiculous number of the creatures.

"My friend, you're brooding today."

Franco's booming bass voice disrupted Eric's latest attempt to shut out the world. He peered at his friend through dark-tinted sunglasses that didn't do enough to screen out Capri's white-hot sunlight.

"I do that a lot, or hadn't you noticed?" Eric replied. "I'm thinking of trademarking it."

"You never used to do it at all."

"It's been a year for brooding, Franco."

Eric's friend sat up on the lounge chair beside him and leaned forward, clasping his hands between his legs. "Have you considered that it might be better for everyone if you approached this Peter Tate about selling out to him?"

Eric raised his sunglasses long enough to glare at Franco. Then he lowered them again and poked his tongue into his cheek. After a moment, he found himself calm enough to speak.

"Franco, my great-grandfather started this business. To sell it to an outsider or to even place an outsider in charge—that would be the last nail in my father's coffin."

"You underestimate your father's strength, and your own," Franco said. "You are young. You could start a new business with the money you would get from Tate. Or you could just live off of your enormous wealth, be a man of leisure."

Eric's mind refused to even process what Franco was saying. "Do you think money and leisure is all I care about? Do you think I'm that self-involved party animal Tate's painted me to be in his magazines?"

"Come, Eric." Franco made a mild scolding noise with his tongue. "You know I do not think that of you. But you must ask yourself—why do you want to keep this business afloat? To please your father? Because you're trying to become your brother? Those are not good enough reasons. Believe me, I know whereof I speak. When I inherited my family's vineyards, I had to learn all these things myself. You will not be able to hold on to Greyford Publishing unless you have some real vision for what the company should be doing. And serving the memory of your brother does not constitute a corporate strategy."

Eric stripped off his sunglasses and glared at the Italian.

Before he could speak, Franco raised a finger to silence him. "You are my friend, and so I must tell you—you are trying to fill a dead man's shoes and it is killing you."

Eric leapt up and tossed his glasses onto the chaise lounge. "Look, I wasn't thinking about Greyford Publishing."

Ironically, for the first time in months, it was true. His whole life during the past year had been a chaotic blur of funeral arrangements, corporate financial statements, festival planning, and more corporate financial statements. On and on it went, until he thought he'd go insane thinking about it all the time. The year had been long and hard, full of sacrifice and compromise and confusion. Nothing had taken his mind off the bitter loss of his brother and the potential collapse of his family's publishing empire. Nothing had brought him any real delight all year—not until he walked into his hotel room two nights ago and found Amanda.

And how had he responded? He'd treated her like some anonymous nightclub pick-up and then tried to force himself on her after she'd already refused him once. *Idiot.*

He glanced out at the glittering blue water of the bay. Directly in front of him, Stacey was trying to teach one of Franco's nephews how to build a sandcastle. He smiled at her determined but rather inept attempts. Very likely, the child could do a better job teaching Stacey, but the boy was too entertained by her efforts to interfere.

Franco came to stand next to Eric, his head tilted at a quizzical angle. "She is a lovely girl, your friend Stacey."

Eric raised an eyebrow. "Off limits, Franco. She's a good friend, and so are you. I'd like to keep it that way."

"What are you suggesting?" Franco chuckled at Eric's obvious protective streak.

"I wouldn't want to see you use her."

"Use her?"

"That's what we do, you and I. Isn't it? Use women and then forget about them. Too many people have done that to Stacey."

Franco shook his head, his laugh deepening and growing, as though Eric had made the funniest joke in the world. "I think most of them know what they are getting into, Eric. Give the ladies a little credit."

Everything about Franco's attitude grated on Eric's nerves today. Perhaps it rankled to hear his own shallow philosophy tossed back at him. "Do you ever want to stay with a woman, Franco?" he asked. "Share every part of your life with her?"

Franco's smile vanished. "No. I made that mistake once, and I will not do anything so weak ever again. Neither should you."

Stacey's lopsided sandcastle collapsed for at least the third time. She threw up her hands in defeat. Turning, she glimpsed the two men standing a few yards away. "Help!" She called out in mock panic, her arms flailing over her head.

Eric and Franco laughed and ran over to her. Eric knelt down beside her in the surf and knocked the whole hideous mess over with one swoop of his hand. Franco's nephew squealed in delight at the mess Eric made.

"That wasn't very helpful." Stacey laughed.

"Sometimes, the only way to fix it, is to start all over again," Eric said.

Franco loomed above him, hands on hips. "My point exactly."

Eric focused his attention on Franco's nephew. "Now, tell us all about your castle. How big do you want it to be?"

As the child spoke, Eric leaned into Stacey. He put a hand on her shoulder and whispered into her ear. "You're just inexperienced. I don't expect The Management ever let you spend much time building sandcastles."

"No, they didn't," she admitted. "But what a kick to discover I'm inexperienced at something."

Franco bent down and picked up his nephew, swinging him in a high arc through the air. "Why don't we give up on the sandcastle for a while, eh? This is not like an American beach. The soil is all wrong for building castles. Let's go to the restaurant and get some cool drinks, eat some lunch. Perhaps we'll think of a better way to build a castle if we eat. I always think better with food."

"That's because you're Italian," Eric retorted. "You think you do everything better with food."

"Only because it's the truth." Franco flashed an insouciant smile. With some consternation,

Eric realized it was directed at Stacey, who beamed back up at his friend.

"I know!" Stacey leapt up, brushing off her hands. "We could borrow some ice buckets from the restaurant while we're up there. We could use them to pack some wet sand and pebbles down really hard. How about that, Giulio?"

Franco's nephew bobbed his head up and down in eager approval.

Eric shook his head. "The vultures are going to be lurking up there, you know."

"Come on, I'm used to them swarming on me."

"I'm not," Eric growled, but he stood and followed the others over to the staircase cut into the rocky side of the hill face.

"Man, that was a good one!" Zeke raved. "Look through my lens. Come on and look!"

He untangled the strap from his ponytail, then passed the camera, with its huge telephoto lens, over to Amanda. At first, peering through it, she couldn't figure out what was so fascinating. She saw a tall, swarthy man with short brown hair, who was swinging a little boy up into the air.

"I see a good-looking Italian guy playing with his kid, Zeke."

"Aim it down and to the left. Look who he's with, and look what they're doing!"

Zeke's voice went up a couple of octaves, he was so gleeful. Amanda shifted the camera lower and then she saw them. Her heart sank. There was Stacey Dakota in a bathing suit so skimpy she might as well not be wearing one at all. Tiny little scraps of rust brown material barely covered her breasts and bottom. Eric's arm rested across her shoulders and his head was pressed right up against hers, as if he was nuzzling her. Amanda's heart gave a sharp lurch. As she watched, the man pointed up the hill, in the general direction of the seaside restaurant where Zeke and Amanda were ensconced.

Stacey stood up and spoke to the tall man with the child. Then she looked down at Eric. He rose, brushing back some errant locks of his dark hair. Turning, he faced directly into the camera lens. The sight of his nearly naked body left Amanda reeling and breathless. His chest was bare and smooth, covered by a network of rippling muscles. A dark, narrow line of hair trailed down from his navel, disappearing into the blue and white color-blocked swim trunks he wore. Every inch of him was tan and toned and perfect, and it could all have been hers last night. If only she hadn't balked and run away. And did she have to get snide and insulting to him on top of it all? *Why don't you treat your business the way you treat women? Geez.* Someday, she'd learn to keep her mouth shut and maybe then she'd find success in her career and her love life.

As she sat under the shady awning of the beach club's restaurant, contemplating her disastrous performance last night, Eric and his friends began to move towards the staircase leading up to the restaurant. Amanda foisted the camera on Zeke.

"I think they're coming up here!" She leapt to her feet and then sat back down. "What should we do?"

"I'll keep snapping away, and you see if you can get a quote from Stacey." Zeke seemed to be in one of his more cheerful moods today. He patted her on the back. "You can do this."

A cluster of photographers and reporters for other publications had been lounging in the rear of the restaurant, at the bar.

"Hey, you guys!" Zeke called to them. "Celebrity sighting—they're headed this way!"

Photographers scrambled to take up good positions for shooting photos. TV and radio reporters gathered up their microphones and crowded near the entrance. A restaurant manager made a vain attempt to quell the excitement but eventually threw up his hands in frustration. Amanda cringed at the sight of all of them swarming into position like sharks lining up to feed. She fervently wished she could warn Stacey and Eric away from the place, feeling nothing but sympathy for their plight.

But then, moments later, when Eric's group strolled into the restaurant, all her pity vanished in a hot wave of resentment. Stacey waved to the crowds of reporters like the old pro she was. She clutched at Eric's wrist and pulled him along beside her. He hadn't even put on a shirt, and Amanda's mouth went dry at the sight of his perfect body so close to her own. At least he smelled of suntan lotion today. If he'd been sporting his familiar scent of sandalwood and cedar while wearing that little clothing, Amanda might have collapsed right at his feet. As it was, she barely managed to pull herself together a few seconds before he saw her. Instantly, his startling blue eyes registered his dismay. In the shady confines of the restaurant, he slipped on his sunglasses and turned away, as if he loathed the very sight of her. The blatant condescension infuriated her.

Damn him and her father and all spoiled rich men. Waving their money around and dazzling women with their designer wardrobes and their perfect teeth. She'd show both of them that Amanda Jackson was someone to be taken seriously.

"Miss Dakota!" She shouted, as she stepped right into their path. "I have it on good authority that your mother will be coming to your show on opening night. Is it true she's also bringing Artemisia Nash, so that you and Mr. Greyford can start planning your wedding?"

A frenzy erupted among the paparazzi, all of them rushing forward to snap photos of Stacey Dakota's stricken expression, thrusting microphones into her face and demanding that she comment. Eric snatched off his sunglasses. His sharp glare cut like a knife and Amanda backed away.

Afterward, as they made their way to their car, Zeke gazed at Amanda with something like awe.

"Jackson, I'm impressed," he said. "I'm a pretty top-notch photojournalist, if I do say so myself. Got my ear to the ground, et cetera et cetera. How'd you hear about that tidbit before me?"

Amanda wasn't about to tell him Dan had simply handed her the story out of some sense of pity. She shrugged nonchalantly. "I have a source."

"Yeah? Well, good work," Zeke grumbled. "You might make it in this biz, after all."

Some days, Amanda truly hated her job.

"That nasty little blonde had to be making that up!" Stacey fumed as she stomped back and forth in the library of Franco's villa. "She looked at me like she hates me!"

"She doesn't hate you." Absently, Eric pressed a thumb to his lips and chewed on it.

"She sure acted like it. Looked very smug, didn't she? I can't believe my mother's going to show up here and ruin my show!"

"She's only going to ruin the show if you let her," Eric reassured his friend. "Refuse to see her until after the closing night of the festival."

"Yeah, that'll be easy!" Stacey glared at him.

"Yes, it will. You are a legal adult now. If you don't want her around, you can have her arrested if she bothers you."

"I might do that." Stacey threw herself across a large, overstuffed divan.

"Have you considered that you should fire your parents and get new managers?" Franco said. He'd hovered on the sidelines in silence, both aboard his yacht and here at the villa.

"I've suggested that to her." Eric joined his friend in front of the huge marble fireplace at the south end of the room.

"Do you think she's bringing a wedding planner to meet us?"

"You know her better than I do." Eric shook his head. He'd look so much more responsible to the board if they heard he was planning to marry Stacey Dakota, of all people. And then, if the two of them denied the rumors, they'd be portrayed in the media as lying phonies, or as fickle and promiscuous and unable to commit. Either image would be unfavorable in the eyes of Greyford stockholders.

Had Amanda made up the rumor in order to get a good story? Eric knew reporters who would do exactly that, but he couldn't imagine Amanda being one of them.

"Stupid, rude blonde bimbo," Stacey muttered. "Getting in my face like that."

Eric wheeled around and pointed a finger at her. "She's not a bimbo. And I warned you what would happen if you went up there, didn't I?"

Beside him, Franco lifted one eyebrow and tilted his head.

"What?"

"Would I be correct in guessing that was your beautiful friend from *Fame*?"

Eric inhaled sharply. He hated the amusement in Franco's voice.

"I should have known from the eyes. They were quite lovely. I take it your evening with her did not go as planned?"

Stacey sat up on the couch. "Wait, wait. What's he talking about?"

"I had a date with that blonde last night. It didn't go well. You're not the one she's out to get."

"Gee, thanks, Eric!" Stacey groused. "I thought you were supposed to be my protector, keep the angry hordes of the media off my back, not get them deliberately ticked off at me."

"Stacey, I'm your friend, not your bloody bodyguard. I am sick of this charade, and I for one cannot wait for the big break-up scene after this damned festival!"

Eric strode out of the room at a brisk pace and slammed the door behind him. He didn't stop walking until he got to the terrace overlooking the sea, where he dropped onto a stone bench.

"That was uncalled for."

Eric turned to see Franco standing behind him.

"I know. I'll apologize to her later."

"That would be advisable. But I think she understands. I am not sure I do, though." Franco sat down on the bench beside him, careful not to look his friend in the eye. "Is the blond why you are in such a bad mood today?"

"Yes. No. Perhaps."

"And this is because?"

Eric looked into Franco's perplexed face. "Women are nothing but a game to you, are they?"

"You have always been a bigger player in that particular game than I."

Eric shook his head and looked away. "It's nothing. She's a nice girl, that's all. It was wrong of Stacey to call her a bimbo."

"You know the Americans and their love of colorful slang. She means nothing by it. She's upset about her mother coming to the festival."

Eric massaged his temples and groaned. "Those two mix like gasoline and a match. I do wish she would stand up to her parents and hire new managers."

"I think she fears she would have no relationship with them at all if she did that."

"She'd be better off," Eric observed.

"Ah, yes, but many of us would be better off not trying to mold ourselves to our family's expectations, don't you agree?"

His friend's implication was obvious but exasperating. Eric rose from the bench and walked over to the stone railing. Leaning against it, he turned to face Franco. "I do care about the company for myself as well, Franco. I didn't become COO solely to please my father and my dead brother, you know."

Franco shrugged. "I couldn't tell."

"I like the notion of the power. I could do a great deal with it, if the company were mine to control. I could take Greyford in a whole new direction, do something meaningful with it. Not publish the same staid European newspapers and a few second-rate tabloids."

"What would you do?"

"What does it matter?" Eric smacked his palms against the railing. "The board would never go along with my ideas, and they hold the real power. There's only one way to fix that."

Franco snapped to his feet and eyed Eric with concern. "You aren't entertaining that idea again?"

"I am. I could use the money my grandfather left me to buy back all the stock. I'd be the majority stockholder then. I could dissolve the board, ultimately even take the company private."

Franco shook his head and folded his arms over his chest. "That is a risky move. If you fail, you don't just lose a company, you lose—"

"Everything I have. I know. And then my father would be devastated. But it's that or let Peter Tate persuade enough board members to vote me out of my position next week at the meeting. He's managed to coax several members to his side."

"Selling out to him would be far less risky," Franco counseled.

As if Eric had ever been a man who balked at a little risk. He remembered Amanda's words on the edge of the cliff. She'd practically called him a coward. A little voice reared up, trying to tell him that wasn't what she'd meant. Only *he* accused himself of being weak. Only *he* would think himself a failure if he walked away from Greyford Publishing and handed the keys to Peter Tate.

He looked to Franco, who still regarded him with an expression of deep concern.

"Someone told me I'm full of fear since Antony's death. What do you think?"

Franco shook his head and waved a hand in a classic Italian gesture of refusal.

"No, tell me."

Franco sighed. "I think you have had a huge shock to the system and it will take some time to adjust."

"Time I don't have," Eric retorted. "Time Peter Tate has used to make inroads into Greyford Publishing. The abominable greed of the man. We're no threat to him. His company is four times the size of Greyford."

"Ah, but he is the sort of man who must conquer everything in his path. Also, you do have considerably more holdings in Great Britain and Europe than he does. If he can gain control of Greyford Publishing, he truly will be Tate Global, eh?"

Eric pushed away from the rail. "Not as long as I have a say in the matter. That man and everything to do with him are utterly hateful to me."

He deserved it. Amanda kept telling herself that as she wore an indelible path into the carpet of her hotel room. He had to know about the imminent arrival of his own wedding planner, for Pete's sake. Didn't he? The image of Stacey's open-mouthed expression passed through Amanda's mind. She'd looked pretty stunned, even—horrified?

Hang on. She hadn't told Eric. The little minx was hoping to back him into a wedding. She'd been planning to surprise him with a double-barreled ambush from this planner and her own barracuda of a mother. No wonder Eric was trying to cheat on her, if she played sneaky games like that with the poor guy. But of course, he was a master of his own sneaky games, luring her up to those woods, then telling her he respected her decision not to have sex—and turning around and grabbing her and planting that last kiss on her.

That last kiss. So full of desperation and longing. She'd sensed his need and longed to respond to it. Ached to do so, in fact.

Her instincts about backing away from him had been correct, though. If a wedding were imminent, she'd have wound up like her own mother. Although her mother had never seemed to resent Peter Tate's absence from their lives, Amanda had borne that grudge for her. And if Amanda had slept with Eric Greyford—well, she'd have had another bitter disappointment to live with for the rest of her life. At least that hadn't happened. She should be rejoicing at scooping everyone else on the Artemisia Nash tip, but the victory rang quite hollow.

~ *Seven* ~

Franco Battali's villa stood in the foothills beneath *Monte Solaro*, the island's tallest point. Outside the gates, on a level plateau, workmen were putting the finishing touches on the big stage where Stacey Dakota and dozens of other artists would perform in the ensuing week. As they milled around the fringes of the stage, Amanda watched a British pop group rehearse for its performance, scheduled to precede Stacey's on the following night. In an unusual move for a headlining artist, Stacey would perform on the first night of the festival and then close it the following Saturday. Her appearance on that first night—or failure to do so—would set the tone for the entire event. That seemed like a risky move, considering her history of late arrivals and occasional last-minute cancellations. Amanda hoped Eric wouldn't be disappointed by the behavior of his soon-to-be bride.

She hunkered down in a seat near the front of the amphitheatre, along with a cluster of other reporters and photographers covering the rehearsals. She'd interviewed the members of the British band before they'd begun to practice. Now she, like everyone else in the press corps, was hoping to see Stacey rehearse. But the British band plodded on, starting and stopping each song three and four times as stagehands adjusted lighting and sound.

"Watching this is exhausting," Amanda grumbled.

"Yeah," Zeke agreed. He barely glanced at her as he spoke. He'd leapt up from his seat and was darting around again, no doubt spotting some compelling image in the glint of sunlight on a bass guitar—or who knew what? Amanda could never tell what Zeke saw at any given moment, although she did have to admit his award-winning photos were always impressive.

Restless, she stood and turned to face the back of the amphitheatre, stretching as she did so.

"I'm going to the little girls' room," said an equally bored Australian reporter beside her.

"Yeah, I guess I will too." Amanda followed the Aussie girl out into the center aisle and headed towards the back, where bathrooms and water fountains had been set up behind a low privacy wall.

Leaning against the wall were Eric and his Italian friend. Amanda stopped in her tracks.

"You coming?" her Aussie colleague asked.

Amanda hesitated, but then scolded herself. She'd done her job in asking them about the wedding plans. Not her problem if Eric had looked at her like she'd stolen his puppy. A lot of nerve he'd had looking hurt anyway. He was the one who'd strung her along on that hillside when his alleged "arrangement" with Stacey involved marriage. And no, she didn't want to hear any contemporary nonsense from him about an open marriage. What was she supposed to do, not go near the bathroom because he was back there? Hah.

"Yeah, I'm on my way." Amanda hurried to catch up to the other woman.

Eric squinted behind his dark glasses. Even with them, the glare off the bass player's instrument at high noon was blinding. Eric usually liked the band onstage and had imagined it would be fun to watch them practice, but now he was thinking he should have stayed at the hotel and listened to their latest CD instead. This sound check and rehearsal had been dragging on all morning and showed no signs of speeding up. If anything, it would run even further behind once Stacey came out to do her rehearsal. The British band merely stood behind their instruments and played, but Stacey brought an entire squadron of dancers and a light show and—Eric shuddered to think what else might be involved. Sword swallowers and lion tamers, perhaps. At any rate, he'd told the stage manager to move things along. Stacey needed to get in adequate rehearsal time, and then they'd all need time to prepare for the party at Franco's house tonight.

As he scanned the performance venue, Franco nudged his shoulder. "Straighten your collar. Your reporter is coming this way."

Eric pushed away from the wall and automatically tugged at the neck of his polo shirt. "There's nothing wrong with my collar." He looked into his friend's laughing face with a dawning suspicion.

"No." Franco chuckled. "I just wanted to see you jump for her."

Eric glowered at his so-called friend.

"I think I'm going to go investigate the backstage area. Have a nice chat." Franco winked and strolled towards the center aisle. Once there, he paused to exchange pleasantries with both female reporters. The man was an incurable flirt.

Amanda and the other woman walked past Eric, chattering and giggling. For a second, he didn't think they'd seen him. Then, after they'd passed, Amanda glanced back over her shoulder for a split second. Through the sunglasses, his gaze met hers, and she turned away again. Eric regarded her voluptuous body with indolent appreciation. She'd worn trousers for a change and flat sandals. Although the combination prevented him from admiring those stupendous legs, it did a more than adequate job of emphasizing the exquisite roundness of her bottom.

He could ask her where she'd gotten the tip about the wedding planner. That would give him an excuse to talk to her. Besides, he genuinely wanted to know. Had she made it up to spite him for their bad date? If not, where had a silly story like that originated? Yes, he would definitely ask her when she emerged from the bathroom. He inched farther down the wall, to where it curved around the back. As he did so, he nearly knocked over the Australian reporter, who burst through the bathroom door in a great hurry, cell phone glued to her ear.

Eric cursed under his breath. This was unbelievably pathetic. Amanda Jackson had teased him and refused him not once but twice. She'd ambushed him with a news story that should have been discussed privately with Stacey and himself. She had no interest in him and no real liking for him. He could have any woman he wanted and most wouldn't hesitate to accept any offer he made. As he stepped back from the door, it opened, putting Amanda directly in his path. She glared up at him.

"There are better ways of meeting girls on Capri, Eric."

"Are there? I'll have to give them a try. Perhaps I could hire one to break into my hotel room and surprise me."

She narrowed her eyes.

"Considering you're getting married, you might want to skip that approach too."

Eric leaned down close to her, catching that clean Ivory soap smell and drinking it in for a few seconds. Then he spoke to her in a harsh whisper.

"I am not getting married and well you know it. You made that up out of spite."

Amanda reared back. Her mouth fell open in amazement. "If you believe that, you must have an ego the size of your Italian friend's villa. As if I've got nothing better to do than concoct revenge fantasies because you left me all tense and sexually frustrated."

She sailed past him and headed back towards the center aisle. Eric squared his shoulders and thought about what the sensible reaction would be. Then he did the opposite and followed her, crowding close to her as she walked. She bent her head down and clenched her hands at her sides.

"I left *you* sexually frustrated?" he hissed under his breath. "I spent the rest of the bloody night taking cold showers and you think *you* were frustrated?"

She stopped short and he crashed into her from behind. She spun into his arms, her chest heaving and face flushed. Dear God, she was so beautiful, it hurt him to look at her sometimes.

"Let me tell you something!" Her voice came out in a raspy, angry whisper. She jabbed a finger at his chest, and he backed away. "If you hadn't moved so slow the other night, I might not have lost my nerve. Then neither of us would have spent the evening taking cold showers!"

Eric's eyes widened in disbelief. "So I'm a villain for trying not to pressure you?"

She balled her hands up into fists and gave a stifled cry of frustration. "Look, what does it even matter? Your future mother-in-law and the wedding planner are on their way here. You had no business even asking me out. And don't give me that nonsense about an 'arrangement,' either. Women who are hiring wedding planners don't make that kind of arrangement."

If he told her the truth, it could easily land on the front page of the next issue of *Fame*. Yet he wanted her to know he hadn't set out to make a fool of her. Eric stilled his protesting inner voice with a few shallow, quick breaths. "Can I speak to you somewhere less conspicuous?"

Amanda glanced all around and only then seemed to realize they'd been arguing, however quietly, in the center aisle of the amphitheatre.

Eric did something out of character, which was getting to be a habit whenever she was near him. He said *please*.

Her shoulders relaxed, and she gave a curt nod. Eric led her back up the center aisle and out of the walled amphitheatre. They emerged in the field that was being used as a parking lot for staff and reporters for the duration of the festival.

Amanda crossed her arms over her chest, enhancing the cleavage displayed by her sweater. Eric massaged his forehead, struggling to banish all thought of laying his hands on those ripe round breasts.

"Look, this is off the record. Does that term mean anything to someone from Tate Global?"

Amanda bristled. "It does to me."

"Fine." He nodded, mostly to convince himself to keep talking. "I'm not getting married to Stacey."

Amanda let out an exasperated puff of air. "Look, our source is her own mother, Eric. She called my editor and said she's bringing this wedding planner to meet with you guys."

Eric ran his hand over his jaw and groaned. Then he walked away from Amanda and sank against the amphitheatre's exterior wall. "I might have known," he mumbled. Stacey had learned all her lessons about wild behavior from a master—her own loud, unstable, attention-getting mother.

"Stacey and her mother haven't spoken in months. This is either some demented attempt at a reconciliation, or more likely, she can't stand being out of the spotlight herself and is trying to wheedle her way back into it."

Amanda took a few tentative steps closer to him. "Is that the truth? Because that's kind of story in itself."

"Yes, and a very sad one. But still off the record." Eric propped his sunglasses atop his head and locked his gaze onto her flawless face. "It's the truth. My word of honor."

Amanda looked down, trying to hide a quiet little smile.

"They have a terribly dysfunctional relationship," he continued. "I think avoiding contact with her is why Stacey's doing so well now. She should get a restraining order against her parents."

He wasn't even half-joking.

"Parents can be a pretty big pain," Amanda agreed. "Sorry if the story has taken the focus off your festival, but you two will get past it. I should go now."

She'd worn her hair down around her shoulders and when she turned to go, it flew out around her like an array of sunbeams. He darted out his hand and caught her wrist. She stared down at it, but made no move to shake him loose. Slowly, he lifted her hand to his lips and kissed her palm. Her fingers relaxed and caressed his chin. Longing for her burned in him like thirst in a desert. Suddenly he was sick of trying to be the respectable businessman. So tired of trying to be Antony.

"Stacey and I aren't engaged. We aren't even lovers."

"You're not?" Her skepticism was readily apparent in her voice.

Eric released his hold on her. "She's like a sister. A frequently irritating sister, as a matter of fact."

Amanda's bewildered expression came as no surprise.

"My brother wanted a hipper image for Greyford, so he signed Stacey to head the festival we were sponsoring. We've known her for years, since we met her at a party when she was a teenager, and we knew she could be rather wild.

So my brother sent me to keep an eye on her, and then the rumors about the two of us started."

Leaning against the stone wall of the amphitheatre, he closed his eyes, steeling himself against the memory of his last conversations with Antony.

"In time, I realized Antony was helping the rumors along, had even planted a few himself. We had a huge argument, and I went off to the Amazon. Then he died and left me with the company and the festival and a star who drank vodka like it was soda-pop."

He opened his eyes again. Remembering hadn't hurt quite as much as he'd expected. Was that a good thing?

"At first," he went on, "I had to watch her like a hawk, because I didn't want to cancel the festival or cut her out of it. She is my friend, after all. And she was a good friend in the wake of Antony's death. I don't know how I'd have made it through the first months without her friendship, and Franco's."

"I wish I could believe you."

Amanda shimmered before him in the sunlight, like a saint in a stained glass window.

"I wish you could as well."

"You've never slept with her? Ever? But you must have kissed or fooled around or something."

Eric shook his head, laughing. "She's done a grand job of cleaning up her act, and I admire her for it, but we're not lovers. Never have been. It was a publicity stunt that got out of hand. Once the train started rolling downhill, I had no idea how to stop it. For one thing, I was too busy trying to figure out how to replace my brother at the helm of Greyford Publishing. Stacey and I concluded it would be easier to stage a break-up after the festival. Neither of us cared about getting involved with someone else at the time."

"How—interesting," Amanda said in a shell-shocked voice. She moved away from him, towards the amphitheatre entrance.

Lunging forward, he laid his hands on her shoulders, stopping her in her tracks. When he leaned forward and pressed his cheek against hers, she sank against him, trembling. "I had something else I wanted to say."

"What's that?" He heard the quiver in her hushed voice.

Eric spun her to face him. "Woman, you're still driving me crazy."

He slid his hands up her neck, caressing the contours of her face. When she didn't pull away, he brought his lips down on hers and wrapped her in a snug embrace.

Amanda's hands went round his neck as his tongue darted into her mouth, teasing and tangling with hers. The heat of her body combined with his, until Eric thought they'd go up in flames together. At last, he broke the kiss, nuzzling her neck and burying his face in her loose hair.

"This is a bad idea." Amanda smiled but pulled away from him. A confused frown creased her brow. "I have to get back to work. And anyway, this isn't the place."

"No." Eric nodded his agreement. "Perhaps later?"

Her eyes widened, and she scurried away from him. Eric smoothed down his shirt and lowered his sunglasses, outwardly cool as he strode back to the amphitheatre.

Damn. Why couldn't he leave her alone? The risk he'd taken, kissing her right outside the concert venue in broad daylight. On top of the false wedding story, a scene like that would get major media coverage.

He was infinitely strange to himself these days. In the past year, he'd gone from a lady-killing adventurer to a harried businessman obsessed with his company's bottom line and its public image. Naturally, the sight of a girl like Amanda made him long for that old, carefree life. But this absurd obsession with her threatened his ability to focus on Greyford Publishing. He needed to get his mind back on the festival, and more importantly, on next week's board meeting. He needed—what did he need?

Bloody hell. He needed to have her just once. Then he could stop wondering about the experience and settle into his new life as a responsible businessman.

Amanda brooded in the passenger seat of Zeke's battered jeep, her pensive mood obvious even to him.

"You act like your best friend got run over by a steam roller," Zeke said. "You should be tickled pink, kiddo. Dan's happy with you now that you dropped that wedding planner bombshell on Stacey D. and her lover boy. She told me she might make their upcoming wedding her cover story."

"Whoopee." Amanda should be celebrating, but she felt petty and slightly soiled. She was also deeply perplexed by Eric's news earlier today. And by his kiss. Okay, not perplexed by the kiss. More like, wound up tighter than a broken wristwatch and ready to go *sproing*. Her lips wanted to believe any tale he told in order to get more kisses like that one.

Zeke cruised to a stop outside the gates of the villa. He handed their press ID's to the gate guard, who instructed them where to park and nodded them into the exclusive compound. Passing inside the gates, Amanda imagined herself as Cinderella arriving at the Prince's ball. To their left, the lower part of a large, grassy hill had been pressed into service as a parking lot and was now filled with the elegant, lavish vehicles of the rich and famous. Zeke parked their nondescript, rust-covered pumpkin between a stretch limousine and a sleek, bullet-shaped silver sports car.

"I'll start out shooting the group photos, then I'll get some individual shots. You can make notes of who's wearing what, who's drinking the most and talking the loudest. Battali will have a pretty huge spread of food in the kitchen for peons like us. I've been to one of his parties at his house in Naples and even the servants ate well that night."

"Nice," Amanda said. "I hate it when we cover those fancy parties and they shoo us away from the food."

"At least it's Capri. No worries about having to settle for a burger at a greasy diner later tonight." Zeke gave a gruff, hoarse laugh at his own witticism.

Together they trekked up the gentle, winding path that led to an elaborate formal garden and a huge, marble fountain sporting a naked sea nymph at its center.

"Impressive." Zeke whistled.

Beyond the gardens stood Battali's house, rising in tiers like a wedding cake, and ablaze with light. Its three levels of terraces were bedecked with small topiary plants and hanging vines. The scent of citrus and eucalyptus hung heavy in the air around them.

"Boy, this guy knows how to live," Amanda mused.

"If I had his money, I'd know how to live, too," Zeke replied.

The low din of conversation grew louder as they approached the terrace surrounding the first level of the house. French doors stood open to the gentle night breeze and hordes of magnificently dressed men and women drifted in and out.

Amanda cocked an eyebrow at Zeke. "We should both have dressed better."

He had, in fact, unearthed something he called a suit. A black jacket that was too long had been paired with a rumpled pair of black pants. He'd pulled his wiry hair back into a ponytail, and to top off his look, he'd added a little string tie like the kind a cowboy might wear in the Old West. The overall effect was that of a dour frontier preacher, come to urge the partygoers to repent.

Impervious to criticism as always, Zeke shrugged. "Speak for yourself, Jackson. You're the one that looks like a waitress at one of the cafés."

Amanda glanced down at her lemon-covered sundress, one of the outfits Signora Claudia had foisted on her. The halter-top bared her shoulders and emphasized her full breasts, while the flared skirt covered up the hips she'd always felt were too big. Although she'd resolved to return the remaining outfits to the signora's shop tomorrow morning, she couldn't bear to give this one back. It suited her body so perfectly. She could barely afford to keep this dress and the one she'd already worn, and she didn't want to be beholden to Eric Greyford for anything.

Her hands went clammy at the thought of encountering him at tonight's *soiree*. No doubt, he'd be wearing the tux again, as he'd been the first time she met him. He'd looked so elegant that night, utterly scrumptious with his tie undone and the faintest hint of five-o-clock shadow on his jaw. If this ridiculous story of his was another attempt to seduce her, she'd never be able to resist. Even now, remembering the smell of him, a mellow heat began to build in her lower abdomen. It radiated lower, and she fidgeted uneasily, plucking at some imaginary lint on her skirt.

Zeke prodded her into the confines of the house, where they found themselves in a huge foyer at least two stories high. A servant noted their press passes and let them know there would be opening remarks in the Grand Ballroom—wherever that was—in fifteen minutes.

"Hey, jackpot," Zeke muttered under his breath as they entered a large parlor. He pointed across the room.

Engaged in deep conversation, two familiar public figures leaned over the punch bowl. One was Jason Everest, a hot new action film star. And—could the universe be this cruel?—the other was Senator Tom Harkness. Her father contributed heavily to the senator's campaign and regularly entertained him at parties. He'd even introduced Amanda to the senator when she'd first arrived in New York, and she'd met the man several times since. Amanda cringed at the thought of being publicly identified as Tate's daughter—and in the middle of a Greyford Publishing event.

"I'll get some photos of them together," Zeke announced. "You can ask Everest about his next movie."

"Later. I have to—um—find the little girl's room." Amanda sidled away from Zeke, who scratched his head and glared at her. "I'll see you in the ballroom."

Pushing through the masses of people, she spotted Judy, the Australian reporter, and a few other colleagues crowded at the bottom of a majestic central staircase.

"What are you waiting for?" Amanda inquired.

"Stacey Dakota," the Australian replied. "She's supposed to be making an entrance any minute—with Eric Greyford. Wonder if they're going to announce the date, eh?"

"I doubt it." Amanda gave an awkward laugh and looked all around at the mobs of people inching closer and closer to the steps. Ever since pouncing on Eric and Stacey at the beach club the other day, she'd been feeling a lot more uncomfortable about this tendency of the media to swarm all over celebrities. Amanda would probably faint if she came down her stairs and found this many people waiting to greet her. Especially if she knew in advance that not all of them were friendly and that some would be pestering her for quotes about stories that weren't even true.

Poor Stacey.

Even as she thought it, Amanda took it back. The young woman appeared at the top of the wide, curved marble staircase, looking serene and in control. She glided down the steps, holding on to the rail but looking up and out and smiling beatifically for the cameras that popped and flashed all around her. Her red satin cocktail dress skimmed her gamine figure, emphasizing her long slender legs and complementing the coppery highlights in her hair.

Amanda and about twenty other journalists watched transfixed as, for possibly the first time in her adult life, Stacey Dakota made an elegant, dignified and completely sober entrance. When she reached the last step, Stacey broke into a wide, child-like grin.

"Hi, everybody," she said to the assembled crowd. "I was so afraid I was going to trip and land right on my bottom. And I bet y'all were thinking the same thing, right?"

Eric leaned into the microphone in front of him and spoke to the assembled crowd, a mixture of drab journalists and society types who dripped with jewels. He was careful to keep his gaze focused on the right side of the room, because *she* stood on the left. Wearing that damned dress Claudia had talked him into buying for her and looking not at all drab. Looking bloody ripe and ready to be plucked from the vine. He pinched his brow and began again.

"The Greyford Wilderness Foundation is a cause close to my heart. The foundation has built sanctuaries for endangered animals in Africa and worked to preserve acres of rain forest in the Amazon. Every penny you've paid to be here tonight will help with this good work, so I'm grateful for your interest and your support."

He walked a fine line when he spoke about the foundation, proud of its accomplishments but trying not to boast. He didn't want it to be seen as some self-aggrandizing *cause célèbre*. Had his brother lived, the foundation might have been Eric's life work, but now it had to take a backseat to Greyford Publishing, much to his perpetual dismay.

We'll have music and dancing and lots of fine food tonight," he went on. "Also some truly excellent wines, thanks to our gracious host, Franco Battali. We look forward to seeing all of you at the start of the festival tomorrow too. And now my friend Stacey would like to say a few words."

A round of knowing laughter rippled through the room at the word friend.

Eric raised his hand for silence and locked his eyes on Amanda's. "Let me add that you cannot always believe everything you see or hear in the media. Take it from someone who was raised in this business. Some irresponsible journalists have set off a round of rather silly rumors, which I hope you'll ignore. Stacey?"

"Thanks for coming, everybody." She ducked a little too close to the microphone and a burst of feedback ensued. A technician adjusted the sound and nodded for her to speak again. "I'm looking forward to singing for all of you tomorrow and again next Saturday. In between my two shows, there's going to be plenty of beautiful music in the fields outside *Signore* Battali's estate. I hope we'll see you there."

Flashbulbs popped in her face and reporters jockeyed one another to get closer to her.

"When's the wedding?" One shouted at her.

"Whose?" she replied with exaggerated innocence.

The barrage of questions continued for several minutes. Dishearteningly, Eric noticed most were about the non-existent wedding. Very few reporters wanted to talk about the festival schedule, even though many of the other musicians were also present at the party. Even fewer wanted to learn more about the Greyford Foundation.

At a designated time, Stacey's assistant stepped up and announced that the Q & A session was at an end and invited everyone to spend the evening dining and dancing.

Eric and Stacey strolled out of the ballroom and into Franco's huge dining room.

"Is she here?" Stacey murmured to Eric.

Amanda had drifted over to a table of cold *hors d'oeuvres* with Zeke, who was stuffing his face like a pig about to be roasted.

Eric gave a surreptitious nod in their direction. "In the white dress with the lemons on it."

"How cute," Stacey said, a trifle dismissive.

"I thought so when I bought it for her," Eric retorted.

Stacey turned on him with a look of alarm. "What are you? An Arab sheikh? You might want to tone down your tactics, Ric, before you frighten the girl away."

"She's already pretty frightened," Eric conceded. "She thinks I'm toying with her. That's why I need you to talk to her."

Stacey thrust a hand on her hip. "But you're *not* toying with this one? That would be a switch for you."

Eric fixed her with a scolding stare. "Toying is not what I do."

Stacey pursed her lips. "You should ask some of your ex-girlfriends about that."

"Thank you. I'd rather not," Eric snapped. "Will you talk to her for me or not?"

Stacey continued to eye him with a look of astonishment. "Are you sure you want me to do this? When we've kept this under wraps for nearly a year now?"

"I don't want her to think—" Eric stopped himself. He didn't what? Didn't want her to think she'd be another short-term affair? To tell her otherwise would be deceitful. He'd never lied to a woman. They knew going into a relationship with him that it would be about one thing and one thing only. If Amanda wasn't prepared for something that shallow, he ought to leave her alone.

Across the crowded room, he saw her talking to the Australian reporter again. She laughed at some remark and then popped a tiny canapé into her mouth. Her movements exuded an unconscious grace that was a delight to behold. She glanced away from her colleague, right into Eric's eyes. He met her gaze and smiled warmly in spite of their public location. Hurriedly, Amanda turned her attention back to the other reporter, but her eyes kept flitting in his direction. She flushed and tucked a loose tendril of hair behind her ear.

Eric grinned, then turned away first, before they both made spectacles of themselves. He discovered Stacey staring at him with her mouth hanging open.

"That's not a good look for you," he told her.

He didn't see why she was ogling him in that way. All he'd done was smile at a pretty girl. Nothing serious.

~ *Eight* ~

All night, he'd been watching her from a distance. Amanda could hardly move without sensing his eyes on her. The first time, when she'd been speaking with Judy, the Australian reporter, Amanda had glanced up and almost staggered back at the hunger in Eric's sapphire eyes. Perhaps it had been a mistake to wear one of "his" dresses; seeing her in it could only add to his possessive nature. And then too, she'd walked away from him this afternoon. That probably made a man like Eric absolutely nuts. It had made Amanda nuts, for entirely different reasons. The yearning that had troubled her since that night on the hillside had never subsided, and his surprising confession had broken down most of the barriers she'd built up in her mind.

Then came her bizarre encounter with the force of nature known as Stacey Dakota. That took care of any remaining reservations.

Amanda had been listening to a jazz quartet down in Franco Battali's gardens. Afterward, she drifted back into the house through the French doors that opened into the Grand Ballroom. Zeke remained outside to take some photos of the party guests in the gardens, which was fine with Amanda. It gave her more time to ponder Eric's story about Stacey. She could always make a conscious choice to believe him and worry about the consequences later. That's what her heart wanted her to do. She wanted to believe Eric was an honest man who'd been forced into an awkward position by his own loyalty to family.

When the jazz group took a break, Amanda wove through the crowd, heading towards the staircase and the upstairs bathrooms. Suddenly someone thumped right into her back with a loud grunt and knocked her off balance.

Amanda stumbled, twisting her ankle in her high-heels. She whimpered and bent down to rub her foot.

The other person squeezed her shoulder and spoke up. "I'm so sorry!"

Amanda looked up to see Stacey Dakota hovering over her. She stood up straight and managed a tight, polite smile. "It's nothing. I'm fine."

"You should get off those shoes and go put your feet up!"

Amanda got the feeling that everything Stacey said would end in lots of exclamation points, probably with little round smiley faces on the bottom.

"Maybe later." Amanda tried to wave the woman away. She should use this as an opportunity to interview Stacey on the spot, but she just wanted to escape from the statuesque singer. Real or not, an image of Stacey in Eric's arms had burst into Amanda's brain and wouldn't go away.

They were so much better suited to each other. How could he not want Stacey? Another spoiled rich kid like himself, Stacey was someone who hung out with the international jet set. She was a pretty redhead with a model-perfect body—slender and leggy, not all round and bumpy and slightly overweight like Amanda. Stacey was also quite tall, Amanda realized as she straightened and tried to stand on her twisted ankle. She was probably almost as tall as Eric. Zeke had once said they made a striking couple, and now Amanda could see he was right. Why was she even thinking about pursuing Eric? Besides Stacey, there were about two-dozen willowy actresses and pop singers and models at this party. Any one of them would be a more attractive match for Eric.

"You should get off your feet," Stacey insisted. She looped her arm through Amanda's and forcibly dragged her towards the huge foyer and the staircase. "Here, at least let me help you upstairs."

Amanda ground to a halt. "I don't need help."

"Yes, you do!" Stacey dragged Amanda forward and pressed her mouth close to Amanda's ear. "I think he likes you an awful lot."

Amanda jerked her head away and stared at her companion. "Who?"

The blood roared in her ears so loudly she could hardly hear Stacey's answer.

"Listen, he's had a few flings since this whole masquerade started, but he never asked me to talk to one of them for him."

"Who do you mean?"

Stacey looked around them. They'd moved into the foyer, and although it wasn't crowded, a number of reporters stood in a knot near the front entrance. "I'd rather not say out loud."

Amanda nodded that she was okay with that.

"He's been a real mope since meeting you," Stacey declared.

"So he sent you to what? Talk me into having sex with him?"

Stacey bobbed her head up and down and giggled. "Basically, yeah."

"He seems to have control issues." Once again, she didn't know whether to be flattered or annoyed. That was becoming a pattern in her relationship with Eric.

"Boy, you've got him pegged all right." Stacey laughed. "Does that bother you?"

"A little," Amanda admitted.

"See if you can work on it with him." Stacey wrapped Amanda's arm in hers again. "He's gotten worse since his brother died. It'd be good if someone could make him snap out of that before it becomes a way of life. You might be the person."

"I thought he wanted you to talk me into having sex with him, not reforming his bad habits?"

Stacey waved a hand in the air. "Yeah, well, he thinks that now. But us girls know better, right?"

Stacey released Amanda's arm and pointed up the stairs. "I'm going to the little girl's room. You?"

Amanda shook her head. "I need to catch up to my photographer. I'll go up in a few minutes."

"Okay." Stacey wiggled her fingers. "I'll see you later. Or maybe I won't. Wow, this has been so cool. I feel like I'm your fairy godmother. Or sister. Fairy godsister! How cool is that?!"

She winked and then scrambled up the huge curving staircase. After she'd gone, Amanda shook herself and massaged her temples. She reeled as if she'd been hit by a high-speed train, one nearly six feet tall and dressed in red satin.

After her unexpected chat with Stacey, Amanda went on the lookout for a chance to talk to Eric. She couldn't decide whether to scold him for inviting a friend to interfere in their blossoming affair—or whatever their relationship could be called. But she knew she was sick of over-analyzing the meaning of their attraction to each other. Whatever Eric wanted from her, she was ready and willing to offer it up. Afterward, she could put the memory behind her and move on with her life.

Over an hour passed before Amanda spotted Eric again. When she did, he was in the company of an Italian opera singer and the dreaded Senator Harkness. That seemed like the wrong time to confront him about enlisting Stacey in his cause. Instead, she went to chat with a couple of fashion designers who'd worked on the wardrobe for Stacey's new show.

"Hey, Jackson." Zeke trudged over to her as she finished speaking with the designers. He was loading a memory card into one of four cameras he'd brought along, and barely looked up as he walked. How he avoided plowing into people was beyond Amanda's understanding.

"Zeke?" she said as he stopped beside her.

"Deadline in three hours."

She'd forgotten all about it. Dan wanted pictures from this party to feature in *Fame*'s next issue. Zeke and Amanda would need to sort through the photos and her notes and get some coherent information together very fast.

"I was hoping to catch up to Jason Everest." At least he was no longer in the senator's company.

"That would be good," Zeke agreed. "Maybe let's go hunt him down and hang out for another hour or so."

"Sounds good."

Together, they traipsed off in search of more celebrities. Amanda was glad to have a new mission on which to focus, but she still found herself wondering if she'd get a chance to speak with Eric before leaving.

Everest kept trying to make a pass at Amanda. Zeke was having a big laugh watching her try to divert the actor back to the subject of movies—or anything that didn't involve Amanda giving the guy her phone number. Exasperated, she cut the interview short. "I think I have all that I need, Mr. Everest," she told him.

"Call me Jason." He leered at her and winked.

"Thanks, Mr. Everest. I have a few more interviews to do. We'll talk another time."

Zeke continued to snicker as they walked away.

"That's enough out of you."

"Kiddo, you gotta figure out how to use what you've got. Men are falling all over you, and you don't even bat an eye."

"You don't fall all over me."

"Sugar, I've got three ex-wives," Zeke grunted. "I don't fall over any woman anymore. But you should be thinking about how you can use this to the magazine's advantage."

"I beg your pardon?"

"Think of the in-depth interviews you could get with some of these celebs, Jackson. Everest was foaming at the mouth for you. And Greyford looked like he was gonna tear your dress off at that *gelato* place the other day."

"I didn't notice."

Zeke shrugged. "A smart girl like you should know how to use what she's got. Man, my wives sure did."

Amanda tapped her foot impatiently. "Do you have more photographs to take?"

"As a matter of fact, I'm going down to the front gates so I can take some panoramic shots of the villa lit up at night," he said. "For my own collection. I don't think Dan's gonna see any value in artistic shots of an Italian villa."

"Go on, then. I'm sick of making small talk with the rich and famous. I'm going to go find a buffet table and add a few more inches to my hips."

Zeke chuckled. "Some men like that, Kiddo. Better watch out or Senator Harkness'll be after you next."

"Go away, Zeke. I'll see you back here in the foyer in an hour."

Amanda drifted out to the terrace and strolled around to the back. The side that faced out onto *Monte Solaro* was much less crowded than the sea side. She spotted a tray of desserts and picked up a small lemon tart. Nibbling at the crusty corners of the pastry, she sat down on a wrought iron bench in a quiet corner. She needed to focus on work, but her mind had been on autopilot ever since her encounter with Stacey. The whole time Amanda had been speaking with Jason Everest, she'd been wondering where Eric was and whether he could see her talking to this renowned heartthrob—and whether that made him at all jealous. How infuriating to want a man this much. She should go catch up to Zeke and return to her room early.

Amanda stood up and brushed pastry crumbs from her skirt. As she turned to make her way back into the house through a pair of French doors, Eric emerged from them in the company of Senator Harkness. The two men spoke in ponderous voices about the need for a global plan to protect wilderness areas. Weirdly, Amanda found it exciting to hear Eric talking that way. She liked knowing that he wasn't the man of his public image—an empty-headed pretty boy who could only think about sex and sports and parties. Amanda plopped back down on the bench and made a pretense of refastening the ankle straps on her shoes, eavesdropping while obscuring her face from the pompous senator.

"Good talking to you, Eric," Senator Harkness said. "Always happy to help your cause."

"Thank you, sir."

"I'd better go track down my wife." The senator sighed, his tone one of grudging resignation.

"Yes, sir," Eric agreed. "Are your daughters coming to the concert tomorrow night?"

"They've been shrieking with anticipation for days."

"Bring them backstage after the show, and I'll introduce them to Stacey."

"Wonderful! They'll be thrilled. See you then, Eric. Tell your father I asked after him."

"I'll do that, Senator," Eric replied.

From her position crouched over her shoes, Amanda heard the senator's footsteps tapping on the marble terrace as he hurried away.

"Enjoying a bit of spying, are you?"

Eric's polished black tuxedo Oxfords came into view. Amanda straightened slowly, enjoying the chance to appreciate his athletic physique decked out in that perfectly tailored tux.

"He's a senator. Might have been worth a good quote or two."

She let go of her ankle strap and grinned up at him. The hard angles of his jaw softened as he broke into a tender smile. He raised a crystal tumbler of Scotch to his lips and sipped from it.

"I can't stand to watch you from a distance much longer." His eyes raked up and down her body, leaving Amanda feeling as if he'd stripped her bare right there on the balcony. And she loved it. She wanted him to make her feel this way all the time—beautiful and sexy and desirable.

"Likewise," she told him, but her voice sounded hoarse and awkward in her own ears. She wondered if he'd noticed. He didn't seem put off by it if he had.

Eric drank from the tumbler again and peered over the rim of the glass, his eyes saying positively obscene things to her. Their message settled deep in her core, where the maddening heat had once again begun to build. She'd never be able to say no to him tonight.

"Here, let me help you with that." He placed his glass on the balcony rail and sat down beside her. Without warning, he swept her leg up onto his lap. Amanda glanced all around in chaotic embarrassment. To her surprise, they were the only two left on this part of the terrace.

"Where did everyone go?"

"I imagine they've all flocked to the Grand Ballroom to hear Stacey sing," Eric replied, running a hand up and down Amanda's calf in a leisurely manner. "Franco persuaded her to sing a few songs with that pianist from the British pop band that's opening for her tomorrow night. She should start in a few minutes. I advised her to save her voice, but Franco's opinion appears to carry more weight these days."

He furrowed his brow and then shrugged.

"I was going to be angry at you for unleashing Stacey on me," Amanda said.

"You were?"

"But now I think it was kind of sweet."

"Sweet, am I?" Eric's eyebrow darted up. As he continued to massage her calf, the strokes became deeper and traveled higher. Amanda gripped the sides of the bench, fighting an urge to throw back her head and moan out loud. Eric's hands slipped under her skirt and lingered on her thigh, making his intentions clear.

"Eric!" Amanda gasped. "Someone could come."

A crooked, conspiratorial smile turned his lips up. "Oh, yes," he agreed. "Someone could definitely come. Perhaps we should move into the library."

He nodded towards the French doors, and then cast an inviting glance back at Amanda.

Her heart beat so fast, it must be audible to him. This was what she'd decided she wanted, wasn't it? To give in to the persistent ache, to simply learn what it would be like with him—and then to part forever when they left Capri. Any smart, modern woman would say yes to this fantasy. Dan certainly would.

Eric hadn't done a rash thing in many months, so perhaps he was overdue. Perhaps that was why he leaned forward and pressed a kiss on her lips, even though he knew anyone could have stumbled upon them as he did so.

"We can always talk for a bit," he teased.

Amanda leapt to her feet, beautiful in her quick display of temper. "Don't start that taking it slow nonsense again. If you're still playing that game, I'm leaving."

She turned, the wide skirt swirling around her and revealing her well-formed thighs. She moved towards the door and placed a hand on the knob.

Eric was behind her in a few short strides. He laid his hands on her shoulders and bent his cheek to meet hers. "I can cut to the chase, if that's what you want." He caught her delicate earlobe between his teeth and gave it a gentle tug.

She sighed and reflexively hunched her shoulders. "Yes, let's cut to the chase. Or even after the chase. I'm so ready for this, Eric. I'm ready for hot, crazy sex and no stupid entanglements. That's what you want, isn't it?"

"Yes, exactly." Strange how his mood plummeted when she said she wanted no entanglements.

He let go of her shoulders and opened the door to Franco's elegant, walnut-paneled library. Amanda stepped into the room and stopped in front of the big leather couch near the door, her movements tentative and uneasy. Eric locked the French doors and then walked over and did the same to the door that opened into the corridor.

Amanda remained utterly still as she watched him. "I've never done this sort of thing."

Only her ragged breathing hinted at the passion she struggled to contain. Her breasts heaved up and down noticeably.

Eric looked into her face, into her wide dark eyes that were slightly wild with excitement.

"You can leave," he said. It was more mercy than he wanted to offer her. He wanted to pounce upon her right here beside the door and strip her naked.

"I won't try again if you go tonight," he added, his pride reasserting itself.

She pressed her hands against his chest. "No, I don't want to leave."

Her hands traveled upward and she caught the lapels of his jacket, pushing it back and down over his arms. At the same time, she tilted her head up, casting a lascivious smile in his direction. Her earlier remarks and her new bold manner made it clear that Eric could be any man right now. She didn't need him; she needed to prove to herself that she was sexy and wild and impetuous. Eric could have told her she was all those things—he'd recognized them straining beneath her naïve facade from the moment he found her in his hotel room.

She gave him a gentle shove, forcing him up against the door.

"Ah, so you think you're taking charge of the situation, do you?" He grasped her forearms and swung her around, so that she was the one pinned against the door. Then he paused long enough to toss aside his jacket and rip off the bow tie. Amanda reached for the buttons of his shirt and began undoing them. He raised his arms on either side of her, imprisoning her between them. Lowering his head, he captured her lips and tasted her sugary lip-gloss along with her own salty-sweet flavor. Instantly, he wanted more of her. His hands spanned her waist, and he leaned his body against her, letting her feel how hard she made him, how much he needed to have her.

Amanda left his shirt half-undone and twined her arms around his neck. Her hands snaked their way through his hair, but her light touch only made him eager for more.

"I want all of you tonight." His hands slipped behind her waist. He tugged at the zipper of the lemon sundress, but it held fast.

"Bloody hell," he muttered. "I should have had her make the damn thing out of tissue paper."

Amanda's laughter poured over him like sparkling champagne.

"You think I'm joking, do you?" he taunted.

She fell silent, regarding him with breathless anticipation. "Depends. What are you going to do about it?"

"This." With animal ferocity, he rucked her skirt up to her waist and tore at the flimsy panties underneath. They fell to the floor in a ragged heap.

Amanda eyed them in amazement. Then she stepped to one side and kicked them away. Her gaze locked onto his, at once defying him and inviting him.

Eric savored the damp warmth of her as he explored further, slipping his fingers into her soft, wet darkness. It had been too long between women, he told himself. That was the only reason Amanda's soft sighs maddened him so. Any woman would have had the same effect on him after all these months.

A little voice tried to argue, reminding him that Stacey didn't make him feel this way; nor did that Italian model who'd been after him for weeks. Only Amanda—

He cut off his own troublesome thinking by taking hold of her arms and stretching them out above her head. Then he laced his fingers through hers and pressed their palms together. "I could take you right here, right now," he said, his voice rough with emotion.

"Then do it." Amanda challenged him as she wrenched her hands from his grasp. She skimmed them over his shirt, stopping at the waistband of his trousers. She fumbled gamely with the fly of his tuxedo pants, but he brushed her shaking hands aside and undid the zipper himself. He reached down, cupping her luscious bottom and lifting her up, positioning himself at the juncture of her thighs. She made a sound of extreme pleasure, like a low purr, and wrapped one leg around him.

"Now the other," he urged.

She eyed him warily. Her previous boyfriends had barely been able to perform on horizontal surfaces.

"Trust me, love," he murmured. And she did. She wrapped her long legs around his waist, trusting that he would cradle her and bear her weight with his own.

Eric plunged into her, and her body tightened around him, greedily drawing him in deeper. As he thrust into her with a relentless rhythm, she writhed in response, smothering her moans and cries against the sleeve of his shirt. Her high heels dug into his backside as her hips arched towards him. Her enraptured whimpers only heightened his need for her. When she sighed and tilted her head upward, she exposed her elegant swan-like neck. He planted kiss after kiss on that smooth expanse and then moved lower, pressing his lips to her exposed cleavage. He refused to let up, wanting to take away every last ounce of her self-control.

Amanda snatched at the back of his shirt, pulling it free and then slipping her hands beneath it, touching his bare skin. Eric shuddered and sank deeper into her. She dug her nails into his back and Eric groaned his approval.

"My love," he whispered, sinking to his knees and taking her to the floor with him.

Amanda sobbed out his name, as she squeezed her legs tightly around him. Then she sagged against his chest, both of them suddenly silent and spent.

A light sheen of sweat glistened on her forehead. Eric brushed it away with his fingertips. When she lifted her angelic face to him, he saw a stray tear roll down her cheek.

"No, no. Don't cry." He lowered his head to kiss it away.

"It's a good kind of crying," she assured him. She drew his head down and captured his lips in a kiss of unbridled passion. Desire overtook him again, and he stirred to life inside her.

She broke the kiss and smiled teasingly, lips parted and eyes half-closed. "You are insatiable."

"Only for you, love." Eric stopped her taunting laughter with another kiss.

"You sweet talker," she sighed.

Eric brushed his hands over the fabric of the lemon-covered sundress. Her nipples hardened in response to him.

"We need to get this off of you." He released her hands and untied her halter-top. The straps

fell around her shoulders and instinctively she
reached up to hold them in place.

"Let it go," Eric told her.

Her hands shook as she pulled them away,
but she let the top slip down for him. He'd
expected her to be wearing some kind of
strapless bra underneath, but he'd been wrong.
When the halter fell away, her bare breasts were
instantly revealed to him in all their glory.

"You are a feast for the eyes," he told her, and
he meant it. As she watched him, he stroked his
thumbs over her nipples and the flesh pebbled
with goose bumps. She caught her breath
sharply and closed her eyes.

Moonlight spilled across the room, casting a
silver sheen on her breasts, her face, and her
pinned up golden hair. Eric pulled the clasp from
her hair and tossed it onto the nearby sofa.
Combing out her long hair with his fingers, he
ached again with longing for her.

"I want that dress off of you," he demanded,
slipping out of her.

She rolled onto her side, so that he could see
the zipper. He yanked it down so violently, he
feared he might have broken it. Amanda gave a
little gasp and rolled back to him. He didn't know
how much longer he could last. Just looking at
her drove him mad with longing.

"Lift up," he told her. When she did, he
whisked the dress off of her.

Eric caught his breath at the glorious sight of
her naked form in the moonlight. The small of
her back was arched up as if even now she were
in the throes of sexual ecstasy.

She gave a soft, breathy laugh, reaching up to
unbutton his shirt. "What about the shoes? Do I
get to take them off too?"

"No, you're leaving those on," he told her. They weren't the pointy-toed black pair, but they were almost as good—white ankle straps with fierce stiletto heels.

"You are such a bad boy."

"On the contrary, I've been told I'm quite good."

And then he went on to show her how true that was.

♡

Much, much later, his head rested on Amanda's stomach and she fingered the unruly curls of his hair.

"Wow, you were right," Amanda chuckled, a throaty, satisfied sound. "No wonder women love you."

He raised his head and grinned up at her. Sitting up, she stroked his stubbled cheek. Then she leaned forward and pressed a slow, gentle kiss to his lips.

Eric sat up beside her and traced the lines and planes of her face. "You're very beautiful in the moonlight."

"You make me feel like I am."

He'd been with beauty queens and movie stars and models, but none compared to her, to her golden hair and big dark eyes and her warm, soft curves. She was like coming home after a long, long journey.

"Well, you are, Amanda, my love."

Even as the words left his lips, a swirling sensation of panic gripped his chest.

Had he actually called her my love? He hadn't used that endearment on a woman since his Cambridge days, when a girl he'd met in a bar had taken it to mean they were engaged. After that, he'd decided it was far too risky and stuck with less emotionally loaded terms like *darling* or even the dreaded and all too American-sounding *baby*. Anything to avoid the implications of the L word.

But now he'd said *my love* to Amanda, and more than once. As they basked in the afterglow, Eric understood what he'd been denying since that moment on the edge of the cliff. Once would never be enough with Amanda. A whole lifetime might not be enough with her.

~ *Nine* ~

Eric pressed his lips to hers again and stroked her cheek. Then the familiar look of grim determination returned to his brow and he drew back from her. She gathered up her dress and covered herself with it, suddenly feeling how naked—and probably downright slutty she must look at this moment.

Eric cleared his throat and looked down, studying his hands. "Amanda, we forgot," he said. "I didn't even use a condom."

She hadn't thought about it at the time. She hadn't thought about much of anything except her resolution to be the New Dan, a bold risk-taking modern girl. Hah. She of all people should have known better. Out loud, she masked her dismay with what she hoped was an upbeat, breezy tone.

"I'm on the Pill," she said. Better not to mention she'd missed a couple of days in the hectic pace since arriving in Italy. "I'm in the clear as far as any other issues go."

"Me too." Eric relaxed and pulled her into his arms. "I'm usually more careful. If anything happens, you'll tell me, won't you?"

His voice sounded soft and timid, not at all his usual gruff, commanding tone. Amanda realized she'd become a member of an exclusive club—women who'd seen Eric Greyford sated and relaxed and vulnerable.

She kissed his hair. "Would you want to know?"

"Yes, of course." He answered without hesitation.

Her heart gave a little leap. "What would you do if that happened?"

He said nothing at first, and her heart settled back into its usual pattern.

"I'd make certain you were properly cared for, you and your baby. I mean, if you decided to have it, of course. I wouldn't abandon you."

Your baby. Not *ours.*

Technically, her father hadn't abandoned her. He'd paid a lot of money for private schools and college to soothe his guilty conscience, and what Eric offered sounded like more of the same. A rich man's solution to a pesky inconvenience.

"Don't worry," she answered, her tone a little cooler now. "I'll be fine." She shoved him away from her, gently but very definitely. "I'm afraid I have to pull myself together and get going, Eric."

His lips quirked upward. "Are you giving me the brush off?"

"I'm supposed to meet Zeke in the foyer. We have to get the photos and text sorted and transmit our story to New York."

Eric stood and languidly stretched his graceful body. His shirt was still unbuttoned and

Amanda watched in fascination as the muscles in his abdomen rippled.

He caught her open-mouthed stare. "What?"

"You're gorgeous. But you already knew that, right?"

Eric smiled and said nothing. Obviously, he got that a lot.

Amanda wiggled into the skirt of the sundress where she sat and only then did she stand up. All this pulling oneself together after the deed seemed even tackier than it did in a bedroom with a guy you'd known for years. She turned her back to Eric as she adjusted the halter-top and reached back to tie the straps. Eric brushed her hands away and tied the bow for her.

"How very chivalrous of you," Amanda joked.

Eric laughed. "I don't think helping a woman dress after you've stripped her naked and had your way with her is part of the definition of chivalry. Unfortunately for me."

She turned to face him as he buttoned his shirt and zipped his fly. She tugged at the zipper on the side of the dress several times before it finally moved.

"Does the zipper still work?" he asked.

Amanda nodded. She'd been worried about that too, what with the way he'd wrenched it off of her.

He walked away from her and picked up his jacket, shaking it out a few times, and then shrugging it on. Afterwards, he strode over to the far side of the room and regarded himself in the mirror as he put the finishing touches on his bowtie. "Amanda?"

"Yes?" She smoothed the skirt down, careful not to meet his eyes.

Eric cleared his throat. Amanda had the surreal feeling he was nervous.

"Your hair is a mess now." He strode across the room to her and reached out, twisting a loose strand around his fingers.

Amanda flinched, not wanting to seem like an easy target again. He'd annoyed her with that cavalier answer about not abandoning her if she were pregnant. She'd annoyed herself in expecting anything more dramatic in his response. She brushed his hand away. "Is that all you have to say?"

"I can't think what I've done wrong," Eric mused. She could hear that sardonic tone in his voice again, the tone he'd used in the hotel room, when he'd made fun of her lack of perfume.

"What do you mean?" She snapped.

"Only that you seem rather eager to get out of here."

Eric retrieved her barrette from where it had fallen on the couch. Without asking, he combed his fingers through her hair and began to coil it up.

"Stop. I don't have time for any more of this."

Eric's hands went still in her hair. "Amanda, let me fix it for you. You can't walk out with it looking like this."

"Fine. But be quick. I have a deadline to meet." Amanda folded her arms over her chest and clenched her jaw.

Eric made a clicking noise with his tongue. "My, so impatient to be gone. You could be a man with an attitude like that."

Deftly, he gathered her long locks into a mass and then twisted it up, clipping it to the back of her head with her yellow and green butterfly clasp. He turned her to face him and studied her, like an artist appraising his own work. Her face heated up and she didn't even know why. He'd seen her naked, for heaven's sake, and now she balked?

"That should do." He nodded to himself. "It's not quite the same, but I think it's close enough."

Amanda looked down. "Thank you."

She started towards the library door.

"Where are you going?"

"I told you, I have a deadline."

"So do I," Eric replied. "In fact, I have to make a business call to London shortly."

He poked his tongue into his cheek and walked away from her, dropping onto the couch with his usual animal grace. "I forgot all about it in the heat of the moment."

Amanda heard shock and even confusion in his pensive tone.

"I wouldn't beat yourself up," she laughed. "You're allowed to take time off, aren't you?"

"What?" He ran a hand over his jaw, calling Amanda's attention to the light beard starting to show there. She'd felt it scrape against her neck, her breasts—all over her, really—when he'd done such an expert job of pleasuring her earlier. Now she looked at the stubble, and her body remembered the feel of it again, the satisfying roughness of it as it had rubbed against her softest, most sensitive places. She needed to stop thinking this way. She had no time to fuss over his moods or be lured by the memory of his sexual prowess.

Yet she stepped away from the library door and peered down at him. "Aren't you allowed to take time off?"

"Not lately," Eric replied. "There's an important board meeting coming up on Monday, and I have to discuss strategy with my financial manager."

He said *strategy* as if it was one of the most hateful words in the English language.

"I think you like being COO of Greyford Publishing about as much as I like writing for *Fame*." Amanda gave him an encouraging smile.

"Yes, in that regard, I suppose we are two of a kind."

"Maybe we should both quit and start our own business." Amanda shied away at the startled look in Eric's blue eyes. *Where the hell had that come from?* It must be that damned cologne of his again. "Sorry. I was only joking."

Eric took her hand in his. He brought it to his lips and kissed her fingers. "You would be a most exciting business partner. In so many ways."

He released her hand and leaned back on the sofa, stretching his long legs and gazing up at the ceiling. "But I'm afraid I'm rather committed to hanging on to Greyford Publishing, dull as it is. I can't bear the idea of selling out to that Peter Tate buffoon. The man's like a bloody schoolyard bully. He buys up smaller businesses for the sheer joy of putting them out of business. All those people out of work at his hands."

Amanda winced, surprised at how much it hurt to hear her estranged father described in that way. *Bully. Buffoon.* She herself constantly railed to Dan and to friends back home about the man's chronic selfishness and insensitivity, so why did Eric's opinion nearly take her breath away? Perhaps because it reminded her how hopeless her attempts to establish a rapport with her father had been. Worse, now she'd added another obstacle to healing her relationship with her father by sleeping with the enemy. Literally.

And what would Eric say if he learned the truth about her relationship to Peter Tate? Since he was still ranting about the man, this was probably not the time to share that information.

"He won't get his way on my watch," Eric said. "I know what I need to do to put a stop to him, and I'm going to do it. That's why I need to call my financial manager."

Amanda bounced on her toes and laughed, eager to change the subject. "There you go, then. Sounds like your strategy is all sorted out."

Maybe she'd never need to tell him about her father. This had been an exciting fling, but already Eric was losing interest in her. She turned to go, and as she did, her skirt flared around her and she felt a cool breeze.

"Where are my panties?" She gathered the hem of her dress tight around her knees.

Eric arched an eyebrow and grinned like a very contented tomcat. "Love, they're for the dustbin now."

He gestured to a tangled bit of beige fabric lying near the library door. Amanda gathered it up and examined the ripped seams.

"I don't have any pockets." She found a trashcan near the mantel but hesitated. "I don't want someone finding my underwear in there."

Eric struggled to suppress a laugh. "I think the maid can handle the shock, my dear. Besides, she won't know they're yours. Unless you put little nametags in them."

Amanda threw the panties at Eric in mock outrage.

He caught them and shoved them into one of the pockets in his jacket, giving in to the laughter. "I'll add them to my collection."

Amanda froze.

"Kidding!" He continued to laugh, the sound deep, confident—and slightly irritating.

"You shouldn't make jokes about stuff like that, Eric," Amanda scolded him. "That's how ugly rumors about lewd photos wind up in magazines like *Fame*."

Eric rose, languid as a cat, and strode across the room, where he tossed the panties into the wastepaper basket. Then he tore some blank pages from a legal pad on the desk, crumpled them up and tossed them into the bin too. "There. Now no one will notice or care, Amanda. The maids have seen far more interesting sights in this house."

"I suppose you'd know. Do you make a habit of ripping up the clothing you buy for your women?" She hoped she sounded playful rather than jealous.

His dimples flashed. "It only happens when I'm extremely—enthusiastic, shall we say? And of course, I didn't buy the panties, only the dress. You'll notice I didn't really damage that." He toyed with the zipper on the side of her dress. Then he placed his hands on her hips and pulled her close. "I take care of what belongs to me."

Amanda laid her hands on his and pried them away from her hips. "Which doesn't include me."

Eric tilted his head slightly, conceding the point. Then he cast his gaze at the face of his impressive gold watch.

That was more like it. She'd steeled herself for a polite brush-off. Eric's post-coital tenderness had only confused her and even irritated her, because she'd suspected it was a polite act. Now his talk about business and his glance at his watch proved her suspicion correct.

"You don't need to worry about my feelings." She walked away from him and grasped the library doorknob. "I understand how this works. We get it out of our system and I get out before I become tiresome."

With the speed and grace of a cheetah, Eric dashed to the door. As Amanda watched, he reached an arm past her and held the door shut. He leaned down and spoke next to her ear.

"You're right. Sometimes that's how it goes. But I'd rather it not go that way this time."

"And do you always get what you want?" she demanded.

"Usually." His cockiness evaporated, and a hard glint came into his eyes. "No. Not always. Sometimes not even the thing that matters most to me."

In that moment, Amanda absolutely knew he was thinking about his brother's death, and it disturbed her. She didn't want to understand him that well.

Eric ducked his head down and rubbed his cheek alongside hers. In spite of herself, Amanda's eyes closed in blissful longing.

His fingertips trailed over her bare shoulders and down the length of her arms. "I was thinking that I wouldn't mind becoming—what was the word you used earlier? *Entangled.* I wouldn't mind becoming entangled. With you."

Amanda let out a long breath and turned to face him, surprising a look of heart-melting tenderness in his eyes. "I'm not sure what you're saying."

This didn't sound like she was being kicked to the curb and forgotten.

"I'm saying I'd like to see you again later tonight. I have that phone call to my financial manager, and I need to bid farewell to a few important guests, but afterward—."

He gave a casual shrug. "I could come to your hotel. I'd invite you to mine, but it tends to be overrun with reporters."

"Is it? I hadn't noticed."

"I noticed. Fortunately." Eric cupped her face in his hands and pressed a feather-light kiss on her lips. "I think I might like to stay."

Amanda pulled away again. She bit her lower lip and remained silent, afraid to understand him.

"How would you feel about that? About me staying all night and us waking up together in the morning?"

The offer intrigued her, no doubt about it. But she hadn't expected it at all. Nor had she expected this gentle, affectionate Eric to emerge in the aftermath of furtive sex in the middle of a glittering cocktail party. She wasn't even sure she liked the new, softer Eric, but he seemed oblivious to her ambivalence.

He pressed his lips to hers again, and this time he was the fiery, demanding Eric she'd come to—well, to really like quite a bit. His tongue plunged into her, invading and demanding a response. She tangled her hands in his beautiful black hair again and pulled him closer to her. He caught her lower lip between his teeth and gave it a playful nibble, then rained kisses down her throat and over her shoulders.

Amanda began to laugh as he continued his ministrations. "Stop, stop!" she said at last. "Deadlines, remember?"

Eric straightened to his full height, his eyes bright with mischief.

"Yes, of course. Deadlines."

He stepped aside, allowing her to open the library door. Once through it, she hesitated. Then she turned to face him again. "The Loreley. Room 237."

He reached for her again, but she dashed away. As she hurried down a long corridor, her mind whirled. Sex with Eric had been fabulous, possibly the best she'd ever had. And that had been quickie sex in his friend's library. What would he be like when he took his time? Her heart quickened at the mere thought of being with him again, but she reminded herself not to get carried away. In a week, this would be over. She'd have a wonderful, exciting memory of her time on Capri, and that was way more than most people got out of life. She'd be foolish to start fantasizing about anything permanent with a playboy like Eric.

At the end of the hallway, she rounded a corner and found herself in the central foyer. Zeke leaned on the staircase railing, chatting with another reporter. When he glimpsed her approaching, he bid the other man good-bye.

"Where the heck have you been?"

"We said we'd meet in an hour," she snapped, self-consciously smoothing down her skirt and checking the tie of her halter-top.

"That means five minutes ago. Let's get going. Last time I drive anywhere with you."

"Hey, it was your idea, not mine," Amanda replied. She looked back down the corridor, a glow of remembrance warming her skin.

"You coming?"

She turned and hurried out the front door ahead of Zeke.

"By the way, your hair's different." He barely glanced at her when she turned to look back at him.

Amanda darted her hand to the back of her head and fingered her barrette.

"The butterfly's upside-down. He's got the green part on top. It was the yellow before. You wanna tell him to watch the details. I knew no woman could resist a big movie star like Jason Everest, even if he is a total jerk with the IQ of cabbage. Thanks for confirming my low opinion of your entire sex, Jackson."

Simultaneously relieved and insulted, Amanda struggled to formulate a coherent response.

Zeke shook his head dismissively. Then he gathered up his camera bags and headed down the winding path to their car.

Franco stole into the library as Eric was finishing up his telephone conversation with Cathy.

"Did you read the samples by that young lady reporter?" she asked.

He had read them, before going to the beach the other day. Amanda had real talent, a gift for weaving a vivid image with her words. That was why he'd been so appalled when she'd confronted them in the beach restaurant. He'd known she could do so much more with her talents.

What if he did hire Amanda to work for him? Could she be his employee and his lover, or was that too unfair to both of them? Would she stay on when their affair ended? He'd hate to lose a good reporter, but women seemed to have difficulty compartmentalizing these things. She wouldn't want to work with him anymore if they stopped having sex. He'd have to choose one or the other. In fact, it looked like he'd already chosen.

"Yes, I read her samples. She's very good." He kept his voice level and nonchalant. "But I think it'd be premature to hire any new staff at this time."

"You're the boss," Cathy replied.

"For now."

Eric rang off and put his cell phone in the pocket of his jacket. His eye fell on the wastepaper basket and he glimpsed a hint of beige silk. He should have kept them in his pocket or burned them in the fireplace. He wondered whether Franco noticed them, then decided he was being too self-conscious. It was ridiculous, since Amanda was certainly not the first girl he'd had on Franco's Persian rug.

A sudden memory of her body, so warm beneath his, threatened to engulf him in a new, futile wave of desire. He closed his eyes and rested his head against the back of the sofa, focusing his mental energy on the company's threatened takeover and the board meeting. Thoughts like that did a fabulous job of dampening all desire, and this time was no exception. When he felt more in control, he sat up and spoke to Franco, who'd been waiting patiently for the phone call to end.

"I've directed my financial manager to buy up a majority of the company's stock as soon as the markets reopen. A sizable majority, one that will give me voting control."

"Some days I wonder why you try so hard," Franco mused, sitting down beside him on the couch. "Is it your chronic inability to accept defeat?"

"Very likely."

"You don't owe this to your brother. Or even your father."

"Antony was always at my father's right hand while I was off rock climbing or exploring or playing polo. I owe them both something."

"Not your entire future."

"It's not only because I want to honor my brother's memory, Franco."

Eric rose and paced across the room to a wall of bookshelves beside the mantel. He'd made a deliberate point of taking himself far away from that Persian rug in front of the couch. Idly, he ran his fingers over some of the leather-bound volumes on Franco's shelves before speaking again.

"I want to prove to myself that I can do this. Not just run this company, but take it in a whole new direction."

"What direction is that?"

"Move away from the magazines and newspapers and start acquiring television stations. Maybe even get into production. We could produce nature documentaries, create a travel channel devoted to wilderness excursions. Produce Internet content."

He took a deep breath and watched Franco's reaction.

"How very grown-up you sound." Franco said, eying him with skeptical amusement.

Eric let it roll off of him. He'd been contemplating this plan for months, but he'd talked himself out of it repeatedly, knowing his elder brother would have rejected it as too risky. His father would be downright appalled. *Television? That's a whole different game*, his father had said to him once when he'd dared to broach the subject. *We might as well open a chain of grocery stores.*

As the younger son, Eric had always wanted to get his father's approval. Succeeding his brother at the helm of Greyford Publishing had been his chance to do exactly that.

Yet in the last few months, Eric had developed the growing conviction that both his father and brother had been wrong-headed in their staid, conservative management of the company. As Amanda had rightly observed—Peter Tate hadn't created his corporate giant with cautious half-measures. He'd been a bold risk-taker. The sort of man Eric had been before his brother's death.

If parental approval meant following his father and brother's management methods, Eric would have to give up on that particular prize. It would be hard to suggest his family's management of the company had been misguided. But it would be even harder to tell his father Peter Tate had bought a controlling interest in Greyford Publishing. Eric could handle his father's reaction to criticism now. Tonight especially, he felt suffused with a bold new confidence. Even Franco's questioning stare couldn't stifle his newfound optimism.

"I can do this."

Franco's expression grew serious. He looked Eric up and down, as if appraising his worth.

"Why?" he asked.

Eric shrugged, not understanding the question.

"Why do you suddenly care so much?" Franco elaborated. "Until now, you've been marking time, eager to get back to the ski slopes and the supermodels. Now you have a vision and the enthusiasm to follow through on it. And you are even willing to defy your father's wishes on how to run the company. Where did this come from, eh?"

"Maybe I want to be a better man, Franco. I want to be known for something more than dating pretty but dim celebrities."

Franco arched an eyebrow.

"In any event, I think this is the way to save Greyford Publishing, and I'm prepared to put up every penny I have in order to prevent it falling into Peter Tate's hands."

His friend said nothing, only smiled with irritating composure.

"Well? What do you think?" Eric demanded after a long silence.

"I think you will be fine, my friend." Franco strolled across the room and patted Eric on the back. "You have the fire of a man in love now. It will stand you in good stead."

Eric bristled. "A man in love? I'm sure I don't know what you mean."

Franco smirked. "Of course I refer to your newfound love for Greyford Publishing. What else?"

"Yes. Of course." Eric fumbled for a conclusion to his sentence and then abandoned it entirely. "I'd better go get Stacey and take her back to the hotel."

"No need." Franco waved a hand in the air. "I had my driver escort her there some time ago. It seems she couldn't find you anywhere after her impromptu concert."

"I might have been on the phone to London," Eric said.

"Of course you were." Still smirking slightly, Franco raised a hand in farewell. "I'll see you tomorrow afternoon, eh? Stacey's invited me to take her to lunch after her sound check."

"Then I'll see you tomorrow afternoon." Eric's smooth demeanor belied the outrageous confusion Franco's remark had provoked. *A man in love indeed.*

Amanda yawned again, even more dramatically than the last three times she'd done it. Still Zeke scrolled through the two hundred photographs he'd taken at the party, contemplating the pros and cons of each individual shot as it related to their story.

"Zeke, I'm getting tired, and we need to transmit the story and the photos in the next few minutes, okay?"

"Do you think we need photos of Senator Harkness?" He spoke as if he hadn't even heard her complaint.

"No, I don't, Zeke. He's not a sexy, young, photogenic senator. He's an old, fat, pompous senator. *Fame* is a glossy mag full of glossy people, isn't that what Dan always says?"

Zeke nodded. "Yeah, but look at this one of him with the Italian model. That's a good one, isn't it? And every guy in America knows who she is from those lingerie ads. She's pretty damned glossy, if you ask me."

Zeke leered at the image in view on Amanda's laptop.

"Okay, let's include that one too."

Every time she worked with Zeke, the assignment ended like this. The man wanted every photo he'd taken to be used in the article—and he always took way too many photographs. Amanda hovered behind Zeke at the little desk in her hotel room. Her entire body thrummed with electricity, and she wanted him out so that she could dwell on that feeling, revel in it. She wanted to stand on the balcony like Juliet and wait for her lover to come to her, not examine photographs of strangers at a party.

"Man, you are restless tonight," Zeke muttered, glancing over his shoulder at her. "That Everest guy got you all wound up, eh?"

"I haven't seen Jason Everest since we interviewed him at the party."

"Yeah, if you say so." Zeke chuckled. "Hey, I'm glad you're learning to use your real talents. Think how proud Dan would be if you told her about it. Not to mention your father."

Amanda glowered at him.

"What? You can get a lot of hot news stories when some guy starts spilling his guts in bed. By the way, where'd you get the tip about Stacey Dakota and that wedding planner? Did you sleep with someone for that one?"

"Zeke!" Amanda stalked over to the desk and swatted him upside the head.

Zeke didn't even blink.

Amanda stomped out onto the balcony and gazed at the café across the street.

"Should I go ahead and hit send?" Zeke called out to her.

"Go on," she agreed. *As if I care.*

After a moment, Zeke joined her on the balcony. He nodded in the direction of the café. "They have good food there. I was thinking of heading over for some late night dinner. You want anything?"

"We ate at the party."

"I didn't eat much. Hard to take photographs if your hands are full of canapés." Zeke nudged her shoulder. "I doubt you had much to eat either, what with being otherwise engaged."

Amanda's face burned scarlet. "Stop it! Go get dinner, and I'll see you in the morning."

Zeke was laughing at her openly now.

"Whatever." His laughter persisted all the way out into the corridor.

As soon as he'd gone, Amanda ran into the bathroom. She hadn't cleaned up since coming back from the cocktail party, because she and Zeke were in a hurry to transmit the article and the photos. Now at last she could freshen up, maybe even splurge with some of that fancy perfume from the shop on the *Via Camerelle*. Or would he like her better without the perfume?

Amanda had restrained her excitement while Zeke plodded through photo after photo. Now all of it exploded out of her like fireworks. Suddenly she was seventeen again and getting ready for the high school prom, waiting for Kevin Dortlander to pick her up in his father's truck.

At least Eric wouldn't be nearly as disappointing as the grabby, inexperienced Kevin Dortlander. She'd tested out the merchandise this time—and she liked it quite a bit. She liked him more than she should, considering his reputation as a heartbreaker.

She decided to skip the perfume, not wanting to appear too eager to please. Instead, she settled for a hasty bath, but no sooner than she'd settled into the tub, there was a knock at her door. That couldn't be Eric yet. Nonetheless, her blood pounded in her ears as she dripped her way across the bathroom floor.

"Is that you, Zeke?" She called as she snatched up her bathrobe. "We are not sending anymore photos to Dan tonight."

She tied the sash around her waist and threw open the door. "I'm not kidding—"

Eric leaned in the doorframe, looking strikingly young in a faded pair of jeans and a plain white tee. He held a bottle of champagne and two glasses. Eying her up and down, he flashed a warm, appreciative smile, full of sex and empty promises.

"Ah," he said. "I'm so pleased to see you've dressed appropriately for the occasion."

~ *Ten* ~

"Is that champagne?" Amanda asked as she stepped aside.

He slipped past her in the doorway, brushing against her chest as he passed.

"Indeed it is."

"Wow, I must be pretty good."

Eric placed the bottle and glasses on a small table near the door. Then he stepped close and pulled her against his chest. "Indeed you are. And I am in a celebratory mood because of it."

"What, you're celebrating me?" Amanda heard herself giggling like a schoolgirl.

"Why not?"

"That could get expensive if we have sex a lot," Amanda cautioned him.

"True. Perhaps Franco will give me a discount on *prosecco* instead. I'll need it, at least for the next year or so."

"You'll need a discount?" Amanda laughed out loud.

"I'm buying back my family's company." He uncorked the champagne. "I've told my financial manager to buy back as many shares of stock as possible. In the end, I plan to buy it all back, but I'll have to liquidate some other investments next week in order to buy more shares."

Amanda smiled at him. "No wonder you're so happy. You're completely in control of everything now."

The champagne cork exploded out of the bottle with a pop, and the frothy liquid bubbled down the side of the bottle. Amanda held out a glass and Eric poured.

"You see, that's where you're completely wrong." His cheeks dimpled and his eyes glowed as he spoke. "This is more like skydiving without a parachute than running a business. This is insane. I could fail spectacularly. If I do, the company could wind up worthless and bankrupt, as will I. Because I'm certainly not going to save myself by selling it to that bastard Tate."

"Are you drunk?" Amanda asked, narrowing her eyes.

Eric put down the bottle and wandered into her bathroom, coming out with a towel.

"No." He dried his hands, looking down at them as he spoke. "That night at the *Arco Naturale*—"

Amanda blushed at the memory.

"I realized later you were quite right. I was very afraid for you. I've been afraid every day since my brother died. Afraid someone else will die. Afraid I'll lose this business that my great-grandfather built from nothing. Most of all, afraid I'd lose myself in the process of trying to save the damned thing."

He raised his glass. "I've never been a fearful person. It was such a new sensation for me, it took a while to identify it. Thank you for helping me do so."

"Oh, Eric," Amanda floundered. Her brain was in chaos. You didn't say things like this to someone who meant nothing to you. Could it be some complicated new seduction strategy? He didn't need that to get her into bed. All he had to do was ask, and she would sink beneath him like a wave.

He tossed aside the towel and closed the distance between them. "I don't want to become my brother. I thought I did, but I don't. He was a lonely man. No wife, no children, no lover. At least, none I know of. All this time, I've been plodding through the days, thinking I had to be like that in order to run Greyford Publishing. But I can't live that way. A man has to take chances or life becomes too grey and colorless and meaningless. Stumbling upon you has reminded me how much I enjoy taking risks."

"I did that?"

"You did." His fingertips skimmed lightly over her forehead, her cheeks, her lips. His hands slipped down, around her waist, and he hugged her against his body. The hardness of him stirred against her belly and a satiny smooth heat simmered up in her.

"You inspire me," Eric said.

He was entirely too good at this. Soon Amanda would believe every honey-coated word he said. Soon she'd believe she mattered to him. As he reached down and untied the sash of her robe, she decided she didn't care whether he was telling the truth. All that mattered was her own longing to be filled up by him and swept away from the real world. No one else had ever managed to make her feel so thoroughly swept away. So for tonight, she'd give his sweet words the benefit of the doubt.

He slipped his hands inside her robe and caressed her naked body. His practiced fingers stroked the engorged tips of her breasts and then moved downward, settling on her hips. Amanda caught the hem of his t-shirt and pushed it up, gliding her palms over his smooth, well-muscled chest. Eric released her and tugged off the shirt, tossing it to the floor. A rush of overwhelming longing flooded her body, and Amanda unbuttoned his jeans. It went far more smoothly than it had in the library. For one thing, he hadn't worn any underwear this time. After all he'd comc to her for only one thing.

When she stroked her fingers over his silky length, he groaned. She grasped him more firmly and he cursed under his breath. "Damn, but you drive me mad."

He tried to pull away from her, but she held tight.

"Stop. Amanda, please."

Relaxing her hold, she flashed a cat-like grin at him. "Do many women get to hear you beg for mercy like that?"

Eric tangled his hands in her hair and pulled her closer to him. "None. Not ever," he answered. "But I promised you all night, and we'll be done in five minutes if you keep doing what you're doing."

His mouth clamped down on hers with an almost angry ferocity. The electric charge from his kiss rippled down Amanda's spine, leaving sparks in its wake.

Afterward, he pressed his forehead against hers. "The more I'm with you, the more I want you. Why is that, do you think?"

"I don't know," she admitted. "I feel the same way."

Eric bent and effortlessly lifted her into his arms, as if she were no more than a feather. She let out a short gasp of surprise.

"I've never been swept off my feet before."

He lowered her to the bed and sat down beside her. "You should be swept off your feet regularly. I should like to be the man who does it."

"That sounds like a fine plan to me."

Eric stood and reached into his jeans pockets.

"I'm better prepared this time." He tossed several condom packets onto the nightstand, and Amanda laughed.

"Very good. You could be a boy scout."

"Love, I'm trying to do the right thing. Don't make fun of me." Eric kicked off a pair of deck shoes and peeled off his jeans, revealing his fantastic tight buttocks and lean, muscular legs.

Amanda's whole body tingled at the sight of him naked and aroused. She held her breath, waiting for him to touch her. He climbed onto the bed and stretched out beside her, nudging open her robe and resting his hand on her breast.

"Stop teasing me," she begged.

"Stop rushing me," Eric retorted. "We said this would take all night."

It didn't, not quite. But it took hours. Hours of the most magnificent sensations Amanda had ever experienced in her life.

At first, they came together with frantic need, neither able to hold back and go as slowly as they'd promised. He thrust into her with the desperation of a condemned man, reducing her to helpless tears again. She tried to hold them back, knowing they'd upset him the first time. She couldn't understand what was happening to her; she'd never before cried during sex. When she told him that, he laughed.

"I don't know whether this is a compliment or an insult."

"It's no insult," she assured him, and so they began again.

After the second, more languid round of lovemaking, Eric retrieved the champagne and glasses and brought them to the bed.

He settled in the middle of the tangled sheets, cross-legged and naked. His confidence in his own gorgeous attributes awed Amanda. She tried to imagine the privileged life that led someone to be so sure of his own attractiveness.

"You aren't self-conscious, are you?" she teased.

"No, and nor should you be." He sat the champagne on the nightstand and tried to wrestle her out of the sheet she'd wound round her body. It turned into an X-rated game of Keep Away, which Amanda lost—or won, depending on one's point of view. They laughed and rolled together in the bed like teenagers who'd discovered sex for the first time. Eric dove under the tangled sheet and parted Amanda's legs, kissing his way up their length.

"How can I keep wanting you this much?" she marveled, abandoning herself to the rising tide of desire and tossing back the sheet.

Eric nipped at her thighs and belly and slithered up her body, nuzzling her neck with another cascade of kisses. He wrapped his arms around her and rolled onto his back, settling her above his belly.

"Condom," she managed to gasp out as she rolled away from him.

Obediently, he fumbled for the packet on the nightstand. She knew it was pointless—they'd both been so careless tonight. Any damage had probably been done back in the library, but this gave them both the illusion of safety and self-control. Amanda desperately wanted to believe she was still in control of her urges. She'd begun this as an experiment, an attempt at being the kind of girl who could have crazy sex with no emotional attachment. She'd got the crazy sex part right. She wasn't so sure about avoiding the emotional attachment.

Condom in place, Eric pulled her down close to him and kissed her again. He twisted her head to the side and flicked his tongue around the rim of her ear. With magnificent grace, he flipped her onto her back. Then he plunged into her until she imagined she could feel him right beneath her heart. She shuddered, every nerve ending quivering as she spasmed tight around the fierce hardness of him. He cursed again and wrapped her in his arms, lifting her towards him.

Amanda cried out, digging her nails into his back. An arc of electricity shot through her and she wound her legs tight around him, squeezing his hips in a merciless embrace.

With one last stroke, Eric groaned and erupted inside her again. "I should have brought more champagne," he rasped. "I wanted to toast you."

A breathy sound escaped Amanda's lips, part sigh and part laugh. "Again? Why?"

"You're the best I've ever had," he whispered as he collapsed against her chest. He slipped out of her and lay beside her in serene silence. Periodically, he played with the long strands of her hair, or brushed a finger over her lips. The blue of his eyes seemed to grow darker as he studied her.

Amanda kept replaying his words in her head. *The best ever?* It had definitely been the best for her, but she didn't have much basis for comparison. Or did he say that to all the women? Perhaps he even believed it—believed each time was the best he'd ever had. If he could convince himself of something like that, it would probably explain his formidable reputation as a lover.

She masked her own insecurity with another display of cheerful teasing, "Are we done so soon? I thought you promised me all night."

Eric nudged her onto her side and then curled up behind her, resting his chin on her shoulder. "I'll give you more in a little while, you insatiable woman. For now, just let me hold you."

Amanda took a shaky breath and covered his hand with her own. "I'd like that."

"Besides," Eric said. "At this rate, we'll use up all the condoms, love. Then we'll have to get creative. Or throw caution to the wind."

"You keep saying you're not a cautious man," Amanda shot back.

"Are you challenging me again? Do you like to aggravate me?" He wrapped his arms around her waist and tickled her.

Amanda giggled and rolled to face him. "Yes, I think I do."

Eric shook his head and gave a short laugh. "Fine. I welcome it." He pulled her over, so that her head rested on his chest. Amanda was filled with such peace and contentment, the kind she hadn't known since childhood. She closed her eyes and slept in his arms.

Some time before dawn, she woke to find herself alone in the bed. Her spirits sank. The whole night had been such a whirlwind, but she'd really expected him to stay. The sexy words he'd murmured to her as he plunged into her body, the sweet words he'd whispered when he held her afterwards—none of it had meant all that much, because he hadn't even said goodbye. Rolling out of the bed, she slipped into her robe and made her way to the bathroom. Returning, she noticed the French doors standing open. Two years in New York City had taken their toll. Now Amanda couldn't sleep securely with open windows and doors, not this close to ground level.

She padded across the room, planning to lock the doors. When she got there, she spied Eric sitting on the terrace, chair tipped back on its rear legs and bare feet propped up on the railing. He wore nothing but his jeans, and those he hadn't bothered to button. As she watched, he sipped from one of the forgotten champagne glasses and gazed out at the nearly deserted café across the street. A quiet smile played on his beautifully defined lips.

"Hey," she said softly as she stepped onto the terrace.

"Hey." He lowered his legs and rocked the chair back into its upright position.

"I thought you'd gone. I came near to locking you out here on the balcony."

Eric smiled up at her but didn't speak. He sat the bottle and glass on a small side table.

"Is anything wrong?"

"Absolutely not." He patted his thighs and then opened his arms, gesturing for her to sit down.

She went to him and wrapped her arms around his neck. Then she lowered herself to his lap. Eric rested his head against her breast.

"I can hear your heart beating."

She didn't know why, but that simple sentence moved her in a way that nothing else he'd said had done. There was such a gentle sincerity about the way he said it, as if he were privileged to be so close to her. Eric drew her down, cupping her face in his hands.

"How much do you care that I'm all out of condoms?"

Amanda smiled. "Not much at all."

Eric untied her robe and grasped her waist. "Turn this way."

He nudged her legs so that she understood his meaning. He wanted her to straddle him, right there on the balcony.

"What if someone sees?"

Eric's hands traveled up and down her body under the robe, setting her libido on high alert. Wet heat pooled between her legs as he touched her.

"To tell the truth, I don't much care if they do," he said. "I don't care if the whole world knows."

Eric shifted his hips and his steely length worked its way free of the jeans.

"Eric," Amanda groaned. "Right here?"

The urge to please him, to please herself, overrode all notions of sense or propriety. It was night on the Isle of Capri, after all.

She rose up slightly and then sank down on him, moaning soft and low as he filled her up and began thrusting into her. In only a few days time, this man had turned her into a wanton sex maniac, willing to perform for him in public under a canopy of stars and darkness. Had he changed her, or had he awakened something that had always been inside her?

"I don't even know myself with you," she whispered as he pulsed inside her.

He stopped moving, caressing her face and tilting it down so that their gazes met. "Don't you?" he asked, his voice so soft she could barely hear him. "I know you. I know exactly who you are now, and I'm not letting you go."

He surged up in her, burying himself deep as she stifled her cries against his neck. She clenched her legs against his hips and rode him to velvety oblivion, finally shuddering to a climax as the first gray light of dawn crept over the *Via Orlandi.*

Afterward, he brushed her hair to one side and kissed her neck. "Amanda," he whispered.

"Hmm?"

"Look at me."

She straightened and peered into those stunning blue eyes.

"A man could quite easily learn to love you."

What else was there to say after that? The look of sheer terror in her eyes made it clear Eric had overstepped his bounds. So many women had wanted his heart, but he'd never had any interest in sharing that part of himself. Now he wanted to give it, but he didn't even know how. Nor whether she would want it if he offered it to her. No entanglements, she'd said—his own philosophy thrown back in his face. Did she still feel that way?

"Eric. Wow. Thank you."

She climbed off of his lap and tied her robe shut, ran her hands through her hair nervously. She fidgeted when she was upset; he'd seen it in his room and at other times. She was doing it now. Wordlessly, she turned away and walked back into the hotel room. Eric followed, buttoning his fly and feeling quite ridiculous.

Amanda ducked into the bathroom and he began to wonder if he should leave. He went to the door and tapped.

"Look," he called out. "I got a bit carried away. Don't pay any attention to what I said. I didn't—"

She threw open the bathroom door and glared at him. "You what? You didn't mean it?"

His heart hurt again. And his head. She eyed him with such blatant suspicion and skepticism. "I meant it," he insisted. "But I didn't mean to frighten you."

Her expression softened. "Oh. Then what does that mean, exactly?"

Eric massaged his neck, not wanting to contemplate the answer.

"I don't know," he admitted. "It means—I suppose it means you've entangled me. And I want to keep seeing you and listening to your laugh and arguing with you and generally keep getting more entangled with you."

Amanda put her head down. Her blonde hair fell forward like a veil, cloaking her face from his eyes. He chucked a finger under her chin and lifted her face to his. Those luscious lips were turned up in a magnificent smile.

"You're such a flatterer."

He wanted to tell her it wasn't mere flattery, that he meant every word. Yet he could see he was making her uncomfortable. Better to back down now, before she became even more skittish. Time would prove his sincerity. There would be so much time for her, once he got past the board meeting and the festival.

Outside, the gray dawn was turning to the full blue of morning. Today was the first day of the festival, and he and Stacey had about a dozen interviews scheduled, plus the sound check to attend. In a minute, he'd have to walk out of here and focus on the business again. And on pretending to be Stacey's devoted lover.

"I really don't want to go," he told her.

"But you will."

"I have to. The festival. My brother's festival, you know?"

Amanda nodded that she understood.

"Do you have a backstage pass?"

She laughed. "Are you kidding? I work for that bastard Peter Tate, Eric. You didn't give any of his people backstage passes."

"I'll leave one for you at the front gate." Eric didn't mean to frighten her again, but he wanted to share his whole world with her.

"Are you sure?"

"I'd like to introduce you to my friend Franco. He'll probably have about two hundred of his closest family members with him as well. They're overwhelming, but harmless."

He saw the hesitation in her eyes again. Yet he couldn't believe it was due to a lack of interest on her part. The way her body answered his, the sounds she made when he was inside her, that crying business. She had to feel as he did, that they'd unwittingly stumbled onto something with the potential for greatness.

"I did already meet him at the party, Eric."

"Right." He nodded, chastened, and drew away from her. "I should be getting back to the hotel. There's a lot to do to get ready for the concert. And I have a rather important board meeting on Monday. I need to talk with my assistant about that."

He gave her a quick kiss on the cheek and moved towards the door of her hotel room. He needed to distance himself, refocus his energy on the business. This was only a bit of fun. He'd planned to teach her how to let loose the pent up passion he'd seen in her eyes. He'd succeeded, better than he'd intended. No sense getting emotional about the woman.

Amanda followed him to the door, tying and retying her robe. The sight drove him insane. He grabbed her hands in his and held onto them. "Will you please stop fidgeting? It's all right. We had a lovely night together and it doesn't have to be anymore than that."

Amanda swallowed hard. "Is that all it was?"

Eric's temper flared and he gripped her hands more tightly than necessary. She whimpered and he released her. "I don't know what it was. It wasn't like anything I've ever experienced. I thought you felt the same thing. I thought you were entangled too."

Amanda wrung her hands together. "I was," she said. "I am. But introducing me to your big Italian surrogate family—that's scary, Eric. That's one step away from introducing me to—"

"To my real family," Eric finished for her. "Yes, I know."

"So what are you saying? Are you saying this isn't just a little island fling?"

"You know bloody well that's what I'm trying to say." Eric hated being pinned down by anyone, hated being backed into a corner. Yet he couldn't deny his own feelings.

"I want to tell you something. Something very important." As she spoke, she twisted and untwisted the belt of her robe. "I'm not who you think I am."

Eric smiled indulgently and held his arms out to her. "I know you've had other lovers. I don't think you're some virginal angel."

"No, I'm definitely not that. But—Eric, I don't want you to hate me."

"Hate you?" Eric cupped her face in his hands. "Good Lord, woman. I'm about as far from hating you as a man can get."

He pulled her close and kissed her again, savoring the salty taste of sweat on her skin, as well as the sweet fruity residual flavor of the champagne on her tongue. Before he could stop himself, he was pushing her back towards the bed and she was laughing, like a queen in exultation. He made love to her again, even though he was sore in muscles he didn't even know he had, even though she admitted she was sore too. Neither of them seemed able to stop it. When she came for him, she cried again, a whole host of tears this time. He kissed every one of them away and promised to return later that night and do it all over again.

After Eric left Amanda, he walked back along the Phoenician steps. The world seemed brand new, and every good thing possible. In her own way, Amanda was as bold as he was. They could be partners in life. His parents were like that; they made every decision together and shared every pain.

Too soon, his nagging inner voice said. *How much do you really know about this woman?*

That voice sounded so much like his brother's. Exactly like it, in fact.

If you were still alive, I'd just tell you to shut the hell up, he told Antony.

But would I? The ghost in his head demanded.

No, Eric admitted. *But I would ignore you anyway and do what I want.*

Yes, you would, Antony agreed. *You would indeed.*

This is big, Eric told his dead brother. It was the first time he'd spoken to this phantom in his head as if it were a friend. *This might have been the biggest night of my life. The stock buyout, now Amanda.*

Amanda made him laugh and yet satisfied his deepest urges. To find a friend and a lover in one package—that was quite a prize, and he'd be a fool to let it slip through his fingers. He wouldn't become his brother, pushing everyone away out of misguided devotion to Greyford Publishing. He wanted balance in his life. He wanted Amanda.

Once, as he made his way back to his hotel, Eric tripped on a broken stair and laughed out loud at his own unaccustomed clumsiness.

A native woman walking in the other direction eyed him knowingly and nodded her head. "*Amore, si?*"

Eric smiled. "*Non so, signora.*" I don't know.

Not yet anyway.

~ *Eleven* ~

Stacey's show was a triumph. The girl sang and danced her heart out and the audience went wild.

"Wow, she's pretty good when she sobers up," Judy, the Australian reporter said to Amanda after the show.

"Yeah, she is." Amanda's mind was a million miles away—or at any rate, it was already backstage. Eric had left the pass for her as promised, and her heart fluttered as she contemplated seeing him again.

"How'd you wrangle that backstage pass, Jackson?" Zeke demanded.

"I've been trying to get one of those for weeks," Judy said. "They told me Greyford Publishing staff only."

Zeke arched an eyebrow. "Learning to use some of those assets to your advantage?"

Amanda shrugged. "I think it was a mistake, but I might as well use it, you know?"

"Right." Zeke shook his head and walked away.

Amanda bade Judy farewell and headed for the entrance behind the stage. A guard checked her pass and nodded her through. "Mr. Greyford's in Stacey Dakota's dressing room. He said you could go right back."

Amanda's stomach churned as she approached the room. The door stood ajar, and she poked her head in timidly.

An imposing woman in red threw the door wide. "Hello, darling, I'm here to help the children plan their wedding! Artemisia Nash. And you are?"

Amanda blinked in surprise and confusion. "I'm Amanda Jackson. From *Fame* magazine."

"Delighted! I spoke to your editor Danielle. She told me to expect you. I'd be happy to do an interview with you any time. Here's my card."

Amanda took the proffered card, dumbstruck by the onslaught of personality from Artemisia. She heard the steady tap of footsteps across the dressing room floor and then Eric's face loomed up behind Artemisia.

"Miss Nash, I believe Miss Jackson is here to see me." He gave the wedding planner a smooth, hollow smile, like a tiger eying its dinner. "Why don't you run along and find Stacey's mother for me?"

Artemisia sniffed, clearly put out by the dismissal. "Fine. We'll speak later, dear."

"Yes, that'd be great." Amanda nodded.

The woman flitted out of the room and disappeared around a corner.

Eric slammed the dressing room door shut and took Amanda's hand. "We can't seem to get rid of her," he explained.

He gestured into the room. Stacey was seated at a dressing table, talking to a small group of people that included Franco Battali and a little boy. She leapt up and approached Amanda with the eagerness of a child. "Did you like the show?" she asked.

"You were great, and the audience loved you. Three encores."

Stacey nodded. "So Eric's been telling us all about you."

"Has he?" Amanda found herself a little frightened by the prospect.

"No, not really," Stacey admitted. "But he's been very distracted this week, and I know it's not my doing."

Franco rose and approached Amanda. "He is right about your eyes. They are quite remarkable."

Amanda looked down at the floor, speechless with embarrassment.

The phone rang on Stacey's dressing table, and she picked it up. After a brief pause, she spoke. "Cool. Send them back. I can't wait to meet them."

Eric pulled Amanda off to one side of the dressing room. "I was going to leave in a little while. Shall I come back to your room?"

"Yes, please." Amanda wanted to plant a sloppy kiss on him as he beamed down at her, but the surrounding audience made her shy.

A knock on the door indicated that soon the dressing room would be getting even more crowded.

Eric cast a glance in that direction and released Amanda's hands. "I'll be right back."

As he moved away from Amanda, she heard Stacey speak. "Hello, Senator Harkness!"

Amanda froze. Her back was to the dressing room door, and she intended to keep it that way for as long as possible.

"These must be your very beautiful daughters," she heard Eric say.

Maybe they wouldn't come into the room. Maybe he and his daughters would say a quick hello and go away. This was no way for Eric to find out who she was. She should have told him sooner. She'd tried this morning, but he'd stopped her mouth with kisses and tumbled her back onto the bed, and then all coherent thought had vanished under his magic touch.

She heard Eric introducing the senator and his daughters around the room, even to the little boy.

"This is Franco's nephew, Giulio."

He would get to her any second.

"And this is Amanda Jackson, a reporter from one of our rival publications."

Amanda issued a short, silent prayer and then spun on her heel. "Senator Harkness. Hello."

"Amanda!" The senator's florid face split into a wide smile. He caught her in a big bear hug—she'd forgotten what a touchy-feely sort he was—and then he shuffled his daughters towards her. "Tiffany, Amber, this is Amanda Jackson. Peter Tate's daughter. You remember Mr. Tate? We were all on his yacht earlier this year when we were at Martha's Vineyard. Well, I certainly wasn't expecting to see you here, my dear!"

The girls nodded disinterestedly at Amanda. They only had eyes for Eric, both of them batting their long lashes up at the handsome, dashing figure standing beside her. At first, she thought maybe he hadn't been paying attention. His demeanor hardly changed at all. He chatted with the Senator and the two girls, and Stacey joined in on the conversation. The girls were too starstruck to say much to her, although one finally managed to ask for an autograph. Stacey cheerfully obliged and then the Senator and his family said their good-byes.

The temperature in the room seemed to drop by about twenty degrees. Stacey sidled away, her head down, and huddled on the small couch between Franco and the little boy. Franco made a painfully deliberate effort to start up a conversation in Italian with his family members.

"That was a revelation." Eric didn't look at Amanda when he spoke.

"I can explain."

"I'm sure you can. Did you call him when I was in the bathroom last night?"

"What do you mean?"

"Your father. You must have been eager to let him know about my plan to buy back all the publicly traded shares of Greyford stock."

"I did no such thing," Amanda insisted. She'd expected him to be annoyed at discovering she was related to Peter Tate. She hadn't expected to be accused of being his spy.

"My agent's acquired better than seventy-five percent of the outstanding stock, you know." He finally looked down at her, his blue eyes hard and glassy with contempt. "Obviously, your father didn't move quickly enough on your information."

"What information? I didn't give him any information!" Amanda exclaimed. "I barely speak to him."

"Oh, that's right," Eric nodded. "I forgot your sorrowful tale of being abandoned and cruelly mistreated by your father. Horrendous mistreatment that included being introduced to senators at yachting parties. I suppose that could qualify as abuse, since most of them are crashing bores. Still, not quite the image you painted for me, is it?"

"He's invited me to a few of his parties since I came to New York. I hardly had any contact with him prior to that."

"Do you know, I don't want to hear the rest of this," Eric said. "I think you need to leave."

Stacey leapt to her feet. "Eric!"

Amanda didn't know where to look. Being dumped by a guy was awkward enough. Being dumped in front of his best friends—that was impossible to bear with any dignity.

"Stacey, stay out of this, please." Eric's voice oozed with silky menace.

"Look," Amanda said. "I get that you're upset. You have every right. I tried to tell you this morning—"

His jaw twitched, as if he would speak, but then he said nothing.

Amanda forged ahead. "We can talk about it later tonight, when you come to the hotel. It's not my fault who my father is. Believe me, I'd change it if I could."

She walked towards the door, fully expecting him to call her back. It didn't happen. Heart heavy with despair, she made her way back to the Loreley and waited for him to come to her. After the passion they'd shared last night, he would want to give her a chance to clear the air.

Amanda waited up all night, but this time when the dawn came up over the *Via Orlandi*, she greeted it alone.

♡

"I can't believe you're holding this against that girl."

Eric sat on the rear terrace of *Villa Battali*, gazing up at *Monte Solaro*. He peered at Stacey through the dark tint of his sunglasses.

"You have a good heart, Stacey. In fact, I've often thought you are too sensitive to last in show business. I appreciate you trying to put a positive spin on the situation, but the fact is, I've been taken for a ride."

He went back to staring at the mountain. Franco had cautioned him about getting too serious. Here was the price for ignoring that advice. It didn't matter. He'd get over it. At least he hadn't blurted the details of his plan too soon, or she might have tipped her father off even earlier. Tate might have decided to alter his own strategy and buy out the shareholders, rather than merely working to turn them against Eric. Water under the bridge now.

Franco strolled onto the terrace and dropped into a chair beside Eric. "I've directed my broker to sell all my family's shares to you, my friend. With your own and your father's, that should give you a total of nearly sixty percent of the total stock. Even if this Tate fellow controls the remaining shareholders, he won't be able to do much to you now."

"I know his type," Eric said. "He'll make sure they show up at every meeting and become thorns in my side. But I'll get the rest of that stock back. One way or another."

Franco nodded his approval, while Stacey paced the terrace and fumed. "I can't believe you threw her out last night. She was so upset."

Franco made a razzing noise with his lips. "The woman was upset because Eric discovered her little deception."

Eric bristled. Although he'd said as much himself, it rankled to hear it from Franco's lips.

"Stop."

Franco eyed him in shock and opened his mouth. Thinking better of any protest, he closed his mouth again and joined Eric in gazing out at the landscape. After a few minutes, he leaned forward, hands clasped between his legs, and smiled.

"Hey, after your big board meeting on Monday, we'll go on a vacation together. You've earned it, right? Two weeks at my chalet in the Alps, and you will be back in good spirits in no time. We'll go rock climbing in Chamonix. We haven't done that in a long time."

"Yes, that would be good." Eric stood up. "I should get back to the hotel. I need to pack for my flight. I want to allow myself time to rest up before that board meeting."

"A wise move," Franco agreed. "When you come back to Capri after the meeting, we can work out the details for the trip to Chamonix."

"I won't come back to Capri," Eric said. "Not ever."

He stood up and walked away even as Franco mouth fell open again.

Eric drifted into the library and sat down on the couch, staring at the Persian rug and trying not to picture her lying there. All her sweet lies about how unsure she was. That pretense of being reluctant. The tears. She'd cried in his arms, more than once. In his massive conceit, he'd believed it was because he'd taken her to some new heights of ecstasy. In reality, she'd probably cried because she was overwhelmed with guilt about being involved with him. She was no cold, calculating Mata Hari. There was too much tenderness in her, too much laughter and gentleness. Her father was a difficult man. No doubt he'd badgered her into seducing Eric and the tears were normal human regret for what she'd done.

You seduced her. The cold, logical voice of Antony again.

No, I did not.

Yes.

Against his will, Eric remembered how relentlessly he'd pursued her. How he'd pinned her against the very door of this room and bent her to his will. How she'd blossomed for him, so eager to please, her appetite so well matched to his own. He *had* seduced her, and he'd hardly even asked her about her life. She'd mentioned her father abandoning her, but had Eric pursued it? No. He'd never bothered to ask her what her childhood had been like. He'd offered her the barest of sympathy and focused all his energy on getting her into bed. He'd even enlisted one of his dearest friends to persuade Amanda to sleep with him.

Eric thought about the absurdity of the phrase *sleeping with him*. He would've liked a night of sleep with her. That one time when she had dozed in his arms, how he'd loved watching her. He could watch her forever.

Except that she had lied to him. She'd made a fool of him in front of Senator Harkness and she'd lied to him. Was she ever going to tell him the truth? Here, he'd been thinking about forever, sharing things he'd never shared with another human being, while all she'd been thinking about was right now. If she'd had any notion of forming a lasting relationship, she'd have told him who her father was. The fact she hadn't proved she didn't want anything long-term from him.

"Eric."

He looked up to find Stacey hovering before him. "Yes?"

"She's here."

He knew that, as a man, he owed Amanda one last face-to-face talk, but the thought of it made him want to punch a fist through the wall. "I'll talk to her out on the terrace. She won't be here long."

"Come on." Stacey traipsed behind him as he emerged onto the terrace and walked around to the front of the villa. "Look how broken up you are. This one's special, don't throw her away."

Eric halted and wheeled on her. "I'll thank you to keep out of my love life."

Stacey clenched her hands into fists. "You're the one who dragged me into the middle of it. And I think you'll be sorry if you dump her."

She turned and went back the way she'd come, leaving him alone on the terrace. He walked slowly, steeling himself for the sight of Amanda in the Mediterranean sunlight. As he came around the corner and saw her, he realized he'd woefully underestimated her beauty and the effect it would have on him.

Amanda stood with her back to him, wearing jeans and flat sandals and a simple white blouse that set off her golden skin. She heard him move and spun around, her blond ponytail whipping around behind her. He longed to go to her and untie the ribbon from her hair, run his fingers through it and forget the last twelve hours.

"Thanks for seeing me." She made no move to touch him or to step closer. "I know you're angry, and you have a right. But I didn't spy on you for my father."

"Perhaps not," Eric admitted. "But you lied to me. Over and over again."

"I never did."

"Yes, Amanda, you did. Every time I mentioned my feelings about Peter Tate, every time I mentioned our rivalry and you said nothing—you were lying."

Amanda groaned through gritted teeth and threw up her hands. "I didn't lie! Listen to me, Eric. At first, it didn't matter who my father was; and then, it mattered too much. In the beginning, we were nothing to each other; we weren't going to see each other again. All you wanted was sex, and I don't even know what I wanted. Something romantic to look back on when I get old, I guess. Why would I tell you anything about my father? He barely exists for me. And later—"

She trailed off and looked into his eyes. Or tried. His sunglasses made it impossible, keeping a reassuring shield between them. She stepped closer to him. "Later, I didn't tell you because it mattered too much. I tried, after that time on the balcony. But you kissed me, and I can't think straight when you do that."

Eric's lips almost twisted up into a smile. *No.* To forgive that easily would be pathetic. She'd lied—or at any rate, she'd kept secrets. But what did it matter? She was right. All he'd intended when he met her was to teach her the joys of lovemaking. He'd done that. Time to move on.

Eric drew himself to his full height and flipped off his sunglasses. "I'm sorry if we both took the moment too seriously last night,

Amanda. The sex was incredible, but that's all it was. Finding out who you are is a reminder of why this should end when we both leave Capri."

Her mouth fell open. He longed to stop it with a million kisses, but he remained rooted to his little corner of the terrace. If he moved any closer, he might smell the Ivory soap and he'd be undone by her again.

Amanda advanced on him.

"*The best I've ever had*, you said to me." She pointed a finger at his chest. "Now who was lying to whom?"

"I wasn't lying, I—"

She tilted her head up in angry triumph. "No. I may not be as worldly as you are, but I know you weren't lying then. You're lying now. I'll tell you what your problem is, shall I?"

He poked his tongue in his cheek and glared down at her. "Oh, please do."

"You're afraid again. You're afraid of what you feel when you look at me. It might mess up the brilliant new life you have planned. Loving me might take time away from building Greyford Publishing into a media empire to rival my father's. Loving me might require you to occasionally put that business on the back burner. Loving me might mean you'd have to be loyal to one woman for the rest of your life, and gosh, wouldn't that be boring?"

No. He almost said it out loud. *No, it wouldn't be boring, if that one woman was you.*

"You are afraid of me, Eric Greyford," she went on. "You're using who my father is as an excuse to put an end to this relationship. You're afraid of what might come next between us, and I feel sorry for you."

She spun on her heel and stalked away from him, her sandals slapping down the marble staircase that led to Franco's garden.

Eric fought down the urge to go after her.

"I heard you two." Stacey ran to keep up with Amanda, who was stomping out the gates of Franco Battali's estate.

"I'm sorry if I got a bit loud."

Stacey caught her arm and held her in place. "For what it's worth, I think you're right." Her freckled face was full of warmth and encouragement.

"I don't know what to say. You've been very nice to me, and we're practically strangers."

"We're two of a kind," Stacey told her. "Both saddled with crazy dads who have way too much power and who've totally messed up our ability to relate to other men. At least, that's my excuse, and I'm sticking to it. Anyway, having good friends makes it bearable, and Ric's one of the best I have. But he's got that macho thing going on, you know?"

Amanda nodded. She appreciated Stacey's kindness, but she really wanted to be left alone.

"Give him time," Stacey said. "I'll talk to him if you want."

"That's a sweet thought." Amanda patted her arm. "I don't need anyone begging a man for attention on my behalf. He got what he wanted, and I guess I did too. It's time for me to close the book on this chapter of my life. It was good meeting you."

She raised a hand in farewell and turned away from Stacey. The gates of *Villa Battali* clanged shut behind her, and she walked all the way back to her hotel in Anacapri.

~ Twelve ~

The London rain pelted down, sheeting the windows of Eric's limousine. The board meeting earlier in the week had gone well, and he should be exultant because of it. Instead, exhaustion overwhelmed him. His energy levels often dipped when he returned to the gloomy English weather after time spent in Italy. He should be heading back tomorrow to watch Stacey close the festival. Instead, he'd excused himself based on the tremendous crush of work as Greyford Publishing's new head. He was a very busy man now.

The driver halted in front of his father's townhouse, and Eric alighted from the car. Climbing the steps with a mixture of dread and elation, he contemplated what he'd say to the old man. His father had slipped out of the board meeting silently after Eric announced he now owned over three-quarters of the stock and planned to take the company private. In effect, he'd told the entire board they would be fired. Some would return in the reorganization of the company, but many of his father's comrades would be gone for good. And what about his father, whose weak heart made every breath a struggle? Had he ruthlessly destroyed the old man's last reason for living? His father had been "out" whenever Eric called these last few days.

"Good morning, sir," Nigel said, as Eric dripped his way into the entry hall.

Eric whipped off his trench coat and passed it into the waiting hands of his father's butler.

"Your father and mother are breakfasting in the small dining room."

"Very good." Eric nodded and made his way down the central corridor. Turning left, he entered the small dining room, so named because it only held about twenty people at the big cherry wood table at its center.

A pert flaxen-haired woman sat at the table, sipping tea and eating toast. She glanced up from the newspaper she'd been reading and smiled. Putting down the tea, she held out her arms. "Darling, I hear you've had an eventful week."

"Rather," Eric admitted. He hugged her and dropped into a seat beside her, looking all around the room. "Is Dad not feeling well?"

"Feeling right as rain," came the gravelly voice from the doorway.

His father stepped carefully into the room. His walk couldn't yet be described as a shuffle, but it no longer had the spring Eric remembered from his childhood. His father was still tall, silver-haired and handsome, but his illness and his eldest son's death had taken their toll. He walked more slowly now and there was a permanent pinched look about his eyes.

"You did a smashing job of taking charge of things on Monday, didn't you?"

Eric wasn't able to read his father's tone. "Is that anger or amusement?"

His father took a plate from the sideboard and loaded it up with slices of bacon and egg.

"Dad!"

A quiet smile turned his father's lips up. "You aren't going to order me about in my own home too, are you? You've rendered me unemployed. Will you also leave me starving?"

"Dad, you shouldn't eat that stuff. Mother—"

"Eric, your father is seventy-five years old. Do you think I'm going to change his eating habits now?" She flipped a page of the newspaper and gave a little exclamation. "How lovely. Harrod's is having a sale. I must call Sarah. No, wait. I suppose I shouldn't be spending quite so freely now your father doesn't have a job."

Eric sighed and rose to his feet. "All right, I get the message. How angry are you?"

His father settled in his usual place at the head of the table. "Not angry. Merely surprised."

"Of course I'm going to include you on the new board, Dad. Did you doubt it?"

His father laughed. "No, you don't. I don't want to be on your new board. I think if you have this bold new vision, you should truly be the CEO. Leave me in peace to tend my roses."

Eric snorted. "You don't garden, Dad."

"Always time to learn."

"Look." Eric leaned across the table and fixed his father with a pleading gaze. "I can make this company sound. I can move it into the future and give it an exciting, unique identity. I promise you, it will be a success."

His father nodded. "I believe you, son. But it's time for me to step aside. You see, I didn't even believe you'd stay on. I half-expected you to come to that meeting and tell us you were selling all your shares out to that Tate fellow. More than half expected it, in fact. Senator Harkness rang me up over the weekend wanting to know what I thought about the impending takeover. Said he'd seen you in Capri with Peter Tate's daughter."

Eric caught the sly look that passed between his parents. They'd always made him feel as if he were an intruder in their private club, and today was no exception. He got to his feet and went over to the sideboard. He'd have liked the bacon and eggs, but after lecturing his father, he felt compelled to choose a couple of muffins and some yogurt. Returning to the table, he couldn't help noticing the merry gleam in his father's eye.

"Is there something you want to say?"

"The senator told me you two looked quite cozy, you and this Tate girl."

Eric struggled to keep his voice level. "Jackson."

"Excuse me?"

"Her name is Jackson, not Tate. She uses her mother's maiden name."

"Ah." Eric's father dipped a piece of toast in egg yolk and chewed thoughtfully. When Eric remained silent, he cleared his throat and spoke again. "I say, the senator wondered if you and Stacey were on the outs. Said you looked rather bedazzled by this other girl."

Eric threw the muffin down on his plate. "You know there was never any real romance between Stacey and me. That was Antony's plan. I merely got dragged into it. Most unwillingly, I might add."

"Yes, before he died, your brother made it quite clear how unhappy you were."

Eric winced. "Must we talk about this? I understand he died angry with me and disappointed in me. I carry that with me every day, Father."

Eric pushed the plate away and leapt to his feet.

His father rose too and laid a hand on his shoulder, urging him back into his seat. Reluctantly, Eric obeyed. He'd given the old man enough trouble for one week.

"Is that truly what you think?" His father asked.

Eric didn't answer. He was too choked with emotion to speak.

"Your brother was proud of you, Eric. Proud you stood up to him and went off to work on that project for your nature foundation."

Eric couldn't find his voice. He'd been so angry all year, knowing he'd let his brother down, knowing his father and brother both had been disappointed in his reluctance to join them in the family business.

"What are you saying?"

"You heard me," his father said. "He was quite proud of you. I was too. I am, son. I can't tell you how proud you made me at that board meeting. You reminded me of the stories about my grandfather."

"Yes," Eric's mother piped up. "Remember the one where he came in and fired his entire senior editorial staff because someone had gotten a fact wrong in an article and none of the editors caught it? Why, you're just like that, Eric."

Eric blinked repeatedly. "I should hope not. That was rather excessive."

"He did rehire them a few days later," Eric's father said. "After he'd given them all a good scare. I admit I'm nothing like that bold and never have been. I've been a caretaker for the company, not a true visionary. Now I understand whom I was taking care of it for. It's yours now, Eric. I will learn to grow roses and you will— what was it you said at the board meeting? *Create environmentally oriented content across multiple media platforms.* I do like the sound of that. Don't understand it one bit, though, do you, Cecily?"

"No, dear," Eric's mother admitted. "But it sounds awfully impressive. Now what about this girl?"

"She was nothing." Even as he spoke, Eric's spirit rose up in protest. *She was everything.* A lilting laugh and a lively mind, her body as intoxicating as any drug. He stared at his plate and said, "Her name's Amanda, but she's Peter Tate's daughter. I didn't know when I met her. She lied to me."

He heard the pettiness in his own voice and knew he'd given himself away. His mother would never let him hear the end of it now.

"About what?"

"About being his daughter."

"I don't tolerate lying," his father sniffed. "Especially unattractive in a woman."

Eric couldn't resist defending her. "It wasn't precisely that she lied. Only, she kept it a secret."

"Now, why would she do that?" his mother inquired. She enjoyed playing the fool, but Eric knew it to be a dangerously deceptive pose.

"Possibly because our family has made its absolute contempt for her father well-known, Mother."

For the first time, Eric wondered if Peter Tate was any more crazy or ruthless than his own great-grandfather had been, than any man would be in founding a dynasty. Than himself.

"What did you do when you found out about her father?" His mother folded her newspaper and put it aside.

"I left her."

"Commendable family loyalty," his father muttered around a mouthful of bacon.

"You left her because of who her father is, something over which she has no control?"

Eric quailed at the piercing look in his mother's grey eyes.

"Not because of that, Mother. Because she kept it secret. Because I found out in the middle of a room full of people, and then I had to act like she hadn't made a complete fool of me. That's why I left."

Although, as he came to say it out loud, it did sound like a gross overreaction.

"Women do have their secrets, Eric. Sometimes for good reason." His mother looked across the table to his father and winked at the old man. "Isn't that right, dear?"

His father chuckled. "You've managed a few grand ones over the years, Cecily."

"Like what?" Eric demanded.

"You, for one thing." His mother picked up another piece of toast and carefully buttered it.

"Me? How was I a secret?"

"We had you quite late in life, Eric. We'd tried for a long time, and we were quite resigned to Antony being our only child," his mother said. "Your brother was ten years old and your father and I in our late forties when I found out I was to have you."

"The plans we'd made." His father shook his head. "You were quite a disruption, boy."

"I beg your pardon?"

"Your father's quite right," his mother agreed. "We'd finally got Antony off to boarding school and were looking forward to being able to live it up a bit. We'd planned a round-the-world cruise when the doctor told me about you. I'm sure I didn't know what to do. I walked around with that secret for a month. Your father had been looking forward to us being alone together again." His mother peered sideways at her father and blushed.

Eric pinched the bridge of his nose. His jaw began to twitch.

"My dear, I was at a loss. I couldn't tell your father."

"But she did tell her girlfriends and a few of the maids as well." Eric's father recalled. "And of course, they all went home and told their husbands and their servants and anyone else they could find. Why, I was sitting in my club reading the paper when Lord Atwell walked up to me and congratulated me on my impending fatherhood. I informed him that he was dreadfully tardy, as my son had just gone off to Eton. To which he replied, *No, Greyford, I mean the new one. Congratulations on the new child.* Quite a shock. Good thing I had a stronger heart in those days."

Eric's mind reeled. "Weren't you angry at her?"

His father laid his knife and fork down on the plate and folded his hands beneath his chin. "I was furious." He gazed at Eric's mother with blatant devotion. "Wouldn't speak to her for days."

"And then?"

"Ah, well. I love her, don't I? She hadn't done anything deeply wrong. Her only guilt was being afraid. I suppose we Greyford men can have rather intimidating tempers. And look how brilliantly things have turned out—her little secret is the joy of my old age."

In a different family, Eric might have hugged his father. As it was, it took him several minutes to compose himself well enough to speak. "I'm glad I've brought you joy, Dad."

"You have at that." His father made it sound like a bit of a surprise.

Eric pushed his plate back and stood. "I'm afraid I can't stay. I have a plane to catch."

"Oh?" His mother gazed up at him. "Where to?"

"I need to go back to Capri."

"But I thought when you came home, you said you never wanted to go there again?"

"I've changed my mind." Eric leaned down and kissed the top of her head.

She picked up her paper and unfolded it. "Very well, dear. Say hello to Stacey for us."

Eric couldn't be sure, but he thought his mother winked at his father as he hurried out of the small dining room.

Artemisia Nash wouldn't shut up. Ordinarily, that was good news for a reporter. It meant Amanda would have plenty of material to choose from later, when she pieced together the article. However, Amanda's powers of concentration had been rather poor this week, and the more Artemisia talked about the many storybook weddings she'd planned, the more Amanda's eyes glazed over. No one knew better than Amanda how rare storybook endings were. Her mother and father hadn't had one, and it seemed unlikely she'd ever have such an experience either.

"Can you turn a little more to the left, Ms. Nash?" Zeke asked.

They were doing the interview in the Augustus Gardens, a stunning, picturesque location. Artemisia said she'd planned and held several weddings there over the years, so it had seemed the perfect location. As Artemisia shifted her position and rearranged her long floral sundress, a shadow fell across their bench.

"Hey, buddy, out of the way!" Zeke protested.

Amanda looked up, but she was staring straight into the sun and it blinded her. As the smell of cedar and sandalwood wafted down to her, her heart began to skip madly in her chest. Her palms broke out in a sweat and she laid down her pen and paper.

"Sorry, Zeke," said a wonderfully familiar baritone voice. "I need to speak to Ms. Nash."

Ms. Nash? Why did he need to speak to Ms. Nash?

Eric knelt down on the ground between them, carefully avoiding Amanda's gaze. He was casually dressed in jeans again, and Amanda thought he never looked better than when he was so loose and relaxed. She noted with some surprise that he carried a small paper bag, which he sat down on the bench between Artemisia and herself.

"Ms. Nash," he said. "I urgently require your services."

"How delightful!" She beamed and clapped her hands. "Wait, aren't you the one who was supposed to marry Miss Dakota?"

"Only in the mind of Miss Dakota's mother," Eric replied.

"That does happen from time to time." Artemisia nodded sagely. "Now, whose wedding would I be arranging?"

"Mine."

Amanda's heart stopped for a split second. He *had* been playing games with her. She'd been a thoughtless last-minute fling, after all. That was why he couldn't even look at her now. He was probably marrying some horsey noblewoman in England, someone who'd bring some additional capital into his burgeoning media empire. She was living her mother's life all over again.

"Excuse me, Amanda dear." Artemisia fished in a huge red tote bag and pulled out a large notepad. "Let me take down the pertinent information for Mr. Greyford, and then we can get back to the interview. I do hate to keep love waiting. Now, when is the wedding to take place?"

"As soon as possible."

Amanda winced. Did he have to do this right in front of her? Of course he did. He was paying her back for embarrassing him in front of Senator Harkness.

"Ah, an eager groom. I like it!" Artemisia began to scribble away. "Do you have a preferred location?"

"Here," Eric told her. "The wedding must be on Capri. I only have one problem."

"Yes?"

"No bride."

Artemisia leveled a blank stare at him. "That's a rather insurmountable problem."

"Not in this case. I have a very specific idea of what I want. She must be blonde, with huge brown eyes the color of melted dark chocolate."

Amanda's lower lip began to tremble.

He still refused to look at her. "And I'd like her to have a spirited temper and a good sense of humor."

Artemisia Nash cast a sidelong glance at Amanda. The look she saw there must have tipped her off to what was happening. She stuffed her notebook back into her bag. "I might have a candidate for you, Mr. Greyford. Can you give me any more detail?"

"Yes, I can. I'd also like her to be a reporter for *Fame* and the daughter of the man who tried to take over my family's business. But most importantly, she must love melon-kiwi gelato."

He picked the bag up and handed it to the wedding planner, who turned to Amanda.

"Miss Jackson, I've only been on Capri for a few days. Do you know of anyone who fits this description?"

Amanda tried to answer but she found herself bursting into tears instead.

Eric rose up and sat down on the other side of her.

Artemisia handed the bag to Amanda. "I think the photographer and I will go off and do some attractive poses near the birds of paradise. Congratulations, dear."

Amanda nodded and opened the bag. She pulled out a container of gelato and dissolved into helpless, tear-filled laughter.

Eric hugged her to his chest. "I do wish you'd stop crying so much whenever I'm around. It might give a man a complex."

"Not you," she retorted.

"No, I suppose not." Eric trailed his hands through her hair and showered kisses on her forehead and neck. At last, he pressed his lips to hers and sighed with pleasure. She tasted of the sun and the salt air. She tasted like forever.

"You came back to me," Amanda said, when at last he broke their kiss.

"Yes. Forgive me?"

"I should have told you sooner about my father. In fact, I shouldn't be trying to keep it a secret. I realized after you left that I've been unfair to him. He wasn't a great dad, but I don't think my mother gave him the opportunity. He's trying now. He gave me this job at his most successful magazine and—as you know—he invites me to parties on his yacht. I should stop acting like I'm ashamed of him."

"I didn't make it easy for you to own up to who you were." Eric stroked his thumb over her lips. After another kiss, he spoke again. "I should warn you I've spent most of my money on taking over Greyford Publishing."

"I don't care about that. You'll wind up on top in the end," Amanda grinned.

"As a matter of fact, I plan on winding up on top later this very afternoon."

"You're very sure of your reception, aren't you?"

Eric's expression grew more serious. "No, not really. That's why I didn't bring a ring. I thought if you said yes we'd pick one out together when I take you to London to meet my parents."

"That'll be fine," Amanda said. "I like gelato better than jewelry anyway."

"I'm not feeding you gelato during the wedding, love. You'll have to settle for a ring."

"Oh, all right." She gazed into his eyes and stroked her hands over his stubbled cheeks. "Are you sure about this? This is quite a whirlwind, isn't it?"

"Amanda, I've known a lot of women and none has shaken up every corner of my life the way you have. I want you beside me while I try to rebuild this company. I want you to be my lover and my partner and my best friend. What do you think?"

Amanda sighed and wrapped her arms around his neck. "I think yes."

~ *Epilogue* ~

Four months later...

Artemisia Nash swept past Amanda, barring the entrance to Franco Battali's villa. The flamboyant wedding planner waved her hands at a knot of reporters clustered in the foyer, as if she were shooing away flies.

"*Signore Battali's* villa is off limits!" she cried. "Come out to the garden, and I'll speak with you there. The happy couple will be along shortly for a photo opportunity."

As they shuffled out, a photographer murmured an inaudible question. In answer, Artemisia threw up her ring-covered hands in an expression of delight. "Darling, they had to come back to Capri. This is where their love story began. And Capri is the island of love, *n'est-ce pas?*"

Beside Amanda, Stacey Dakota stifled a snort. "*N'est-ce pas?* Why does she talk that way? Isn't she from Cleveland?"

Amanda giggled. "Yes, but I can't argue with a woman's desire to re-invent herself, can you?"

"No," Stacey agreed.

"Besides, she does plan a beautiful wedding." Amanda tugged at the chapel train of her gown, trying to push it behind her.

"Here, let me. My job, after all." Stacey knelt down, no easy task in her blue, sheath-style bridesmaid dress. She carefully fanned the train behind Amanda.

"That looks great." Zeke shambled into the foyer with a camera and tripod. "Make her stand still like that so I can get a couple of good portrait photos."

Stacey nodded and rose to her full height beside Amanda.

"I guess it's a good thing Artemisia works fast too," she whispered.

Amanda ears flushed red. "Yes, it is. I can hardly fit into the dress now. And I want to go to the Rain Forest before I'm too fat and pregnant to enjoy it."

"That doesn't sound like much of a honeymoon to me."

"We're going to spend two weeks on the beach in Brazil first, for the non-working portion of the honeymoon," Amanda explained.

"Is Eric okay with you going to the Amazon in your condition? Isn't he worried about your safety?"

The women turned and peered across the corridor, where Eric was surrounded by a cluster of laughing, backslapping groomsmen. As though he sensed Amanda's eyes on him, he turned from them to meet her gaze. His chest swelled, and a wide smile brightened his handsome face. He made a brief remark to his companions, and then made his way to her through the crowd.

"Hello, Mrs. Greyford." He brushed his lips against her cheek and pulled her backwards against his chest, totally disarranging her train once again. She snuggled into his ready embrace, flooded with a feeling of supreme joy.

Across the foyer, Zeke muttered a few choice curse words and put his camera down.

"Give us a minute, Zeke," Amanda called to him.

He rolled his eyes but stood patiently off to the side.

"How are you, Stacey?" Eric asked.

"Doing great."

"You and your mom getting along okay?" Amanda asked.

"We are," Stacey nodded. "We argue a lot less now that we're mother and daughter and not manager and client. My dad took being fired pretty hard, though. He still won't speak to me. I suppose it doesn't help that my mom's finally decided to file for divorce."

"Considering their constant bickering, I think they'll both be better off."

"I do too," Stacey agreed. "Mom's been very happy and relaxed. We went shopping together for your wedding present yesterday."

"Good, good," Eric nodded and brushed his lips against Amanda's cheek again. She could tell he didn't care what anyone was saying to him right now. As he drew her against him, she could feel that he was quite ready for the honeymoon to begin.

Amanda struggled to keep her mind on social niceties. "How are things with Franco?"

Stacey shrugged. "He's a good guy. I don't think we're going off on a hasty wedding and honeymoon, though. I think he's still carrying a torch for someone else."

Amanda leaned away from Eric and grinned up at him. "That's what Eric keeps saying."

"It's all right," Stacey insisted. "We enjoy each other's company. And he has such a great family. I'm mostly dating him for the ready access to all that fine Italian food."

They were still laughing together when Amanda's father approached them.

"Greyford." He nodded stiffly at Eric, who responded in kind.

"You two," Amanda sighed. "Dad, at least shake his hand."

"Why should I, when he keeps robbing me of all the best prizes? Bad enough he's marrying you. Did he have to hire you away to write nature documentaries?"

He frowned at the glass he was holding. Amanda found herself touched by his gruff display of affection. She pried herself free of Eric's embrace and patted her father's cheek. "I appreciate you being here to give me away."

"Had to rearrange a board meeting to do it," Peter Tate muttered. "I'm trying."

"I know you are," Amanda nodded. She stepped back into Eric's waiting arms.

"Greyford, are you quite sure about taking her to the Amazon with you?"

"We've been over all of this, Mr. Tate," Eric sighed. "It's not like we're going to be living all that rough. Amanda and I will only be there for a month, and we've got a doctor and nurse on the team. And no doubt you'll flit in via helicopter for the occasional annoying, unexpected visit."

Amanda's father harrumphed and swirled his drink. "Want to know I'm getting my money's worth out of this joint venture. Greyford may be producing the documentary but Tate Global's going to be airing the thing on my American television stations. Hope I don't regret letting Amanda talk me into this project."

"You won't," Eric retorted. "I know what I'm doing."

Peter Tate cast a stern, appraising look at Eric. "Yes, I think you do. You remind me of myself at your age."

Eric's eyes widened in mock horror. "Good God, do I?"

The older man chuckled. "No. You're much smarter. Congratulations."

He thrust a hand out to Eric, gave him a quick, sharp shake, and then turned to Stacey.

"Where's that mother of yours? Quite an attractive woman. I can see where you get your good looks."

Stacey laughed. "I think she's out on the terrace. I'll help you find her."

She waved to Eric and Amanda, and then strolled away with Peter Tate. Zeke had been lounging against the banister of the central staircase and straightened hopefully.

"All right, Zeke," Eric called to him. "But be quick. I need to kiss my bride."

"Go right ahead," Zeke shot back. "I'm a pretty good action photographer." His hangdog face broke into a melancholy smile.

Eric swept Amanda into his arms and Amanda beamed up at him, her heart bursting with joy at how well everything had turned out. Eric loved her. He hadn't even batted an eye when she'd told him about the baby. He'd swung her into the air and whooped with excitement that day. She'd made a wonderful new friend in Stacey Dakota. And even her relationship with her father was improving. Life didn't get much better than this.

"Happy, Mrs. Greyford?"

"Ecstatic, Mr. Greyford," Amanda answered.

Eric captured her lips in a kiss that was full of tenderness and passion. When at last they parted, they discovered the assembled guests crowded into the foyer, cheering and applauding.

Artemisia Nash appeared in the foyer doorway. "That was beautiful, children. Now let's go out to the garden for your public debut as man and wife."

She extended a hand, chauffeuring them out the door.

Eric smiled down at Amanda.

"I'm ready. You?"

"Oh, yes." Amanda nodded.

Eric took her hand and together they walked out of the *Villa Battali* and into the first morning of the rest of their life.

The Beginning

Thank you for reading *Love, Capri Style*. Please turn the page for an excerpt from *Thirty-Nine Again*, Lynn Reynolds' chick noir suspense novel. *RT Book Reviews* called it "a first class mystery...and a first-class read."

Thirty-Nine Again
a "chick noir" novel

by

Lynn Reynolds

What's chick noir? It's like chick lit, but with guns and dead bodies instead of shoes...

On her first thirty-ninth birthday, Sabrina O'Hara battled cancer. This year, she discovers her fiancé Scott's leading a treacherous double life. Now she's on the run—from Scott, from the Mexican Mafia, and from one dangerously sexy Homeland Security Agent. Thirty-nine the first time was horrible. But can Sabrina survive Thirty-Nine Again?

RT Book Reviews said: 4 Stars
"[*Thirty-Nine Again* is] a first-class mystery and...a first-class read."

~ ~ ~

Chapter One

The day of my second thirty-ninth birthday began beautifully, but that just goes to show you appearances can be deceiving. Overnight, the unseasonably mild autumn had blossomed into full-fledged spring, with sunshine and temperatures expected to reach the seventies. All day, childish glee bubbled in me at the realization I'd lived to see another birthday. It bubbled even bigger as the workday drew to a close—I had planned to knock off work early to run with Evan down at Harborplace.

I blew off the gang at the office, even though they wanted to take me to Pazo to celebrate. Because I'd had no energy for celebrating my first thirty-ninth birthday—chemotherapy and radiation treatments will do that to a person—they'd wanted to make it up to me this year. I felt a little bad when I broke the news, but they weren't too put out about it. In fact, a round of cheering went up. Everyone knew Scott and I had been drifting apart, so they were kind of pleased to hear someone else had inched into the picture. I denied that was the case, of course, even to myself.

"Evan's just helping me get back into shape after surgery. He's my new personal trainer, and he figured I'd stick with running more regularly if I had a partner."

"I'll bet he can think of a few other things you'll do better with a partner, too!" laughed Andy from Information Services.

"Not true!" My friend Jess winked at him. "Sabrina says he's gay."

"Really?" Andy's interest wasn't all that altruistic. He's gay, and he'd seen Evan once when we ran into him in Starbucks. "Are you sure?"

As a matter of fact, I wasn't. I had never said I was sure. I'd only mentioned it in passing, a point of curiosity because of the whole earring thing. He wore earrings in both ears, and I was old enough to remember a time when only gay guys did that. But Jess and Andy reminded me that wasn't the case anymore.

How does someone know when a cultural shift like that takes place? How, as a straight guy, would you know it's now safe to wear earrings in both ears? I mean, even Bono has earrings in both ears now, and he's got something like sixty-seven kids, doesn't he? When did he get the memo?

"No, I'm not sure Evan is gay," I admitted.

"Mmm-hmm," from both of them.

"Cut it out. If he is straight or bi or whatever, it doesn't matter. I'm sure I'm too frumpy for the likes of him."

"Oh, girl, have you looked in a mirror lately?" Jess sighed.

Of course I hadn't, not closely anyway. I avoided mirrors as much as possible. First, I'd been a chubby, freckle faced teen, then last year I'd been bald. Now I was missing a sizable part of one breast—euphemistically called a lumpectomy. Bottom line, mirrors had never been my friends.

"I have to go." I snatched up my gym bag. "I'll try to come to the restaurant later tonight."

"You'll try?!" Andy shook with laughter. "You'll try? You mean, if you aren't too worn out from all that running?"

"We won't hold our breath," Jess added.

I exited to the sound of clapping and a lot of ribald whistling.

Evan and I were supposed to meet at the amphitheatre in front of the harbor, but when I arrived, I saw no sign of him. I wondered if I was late or maybe he changed his mind, and I paced around nervously. Then I decided I shouldn't look too interested, so I strolled over to the angled steps near the water taxi's passenger loading area. I sat down and further decided my left shoelace was too tight and my right shoelace was too loose. So I untied them both and began to retie them.

Evan jogged around a corner and stopped beside me. "Hey, I thought maybe you decided not to come!"

I looked up, disappointed to discover his dark eyes were hidden by a pair of those Oakley sunglasses that big with military guys.

"Ready to go?"

"Yeah, sure!" I felt my face heating up involuntarily and heard the perky little exclamation point in my voice. It made me ill.

I charged up the steps to cover my own embarrassment, but I'd never finished with the whole shoelace-tying thing, so I got tangled in my own feet and stumbled. Badly. I stumbled in a way only I could stumble. I started to fall face forward right into Evan's arms. That threw me into such a huge panic that I windmilled my arms wildly and tried to arch away from him. I flailed backwards, somersaulting down the steps and coming within a millimeter of rolling into the dirty, oily water of the harbor. The only thing that saved me was Evan, who dove down the steps with incredible speed and grabbed me by the arms. I wound up with my legs in the water but my clothes unscathed. He pulled me onto the steps, and I buried my face in my hands.

"Oh, that went way better than the gym," I muttered.

Evan snorted, blatantly failing to hide his amusement. "Are you okay?"

"No," I replied. "I am not. I have a bloody knee that's probably been exposed to all sorts of mutant flesh-eating bacteria. And my pride is utterly in tatters."

"Not to worry." He left me there and jogged over to the Light Street Pavilion, the one with all the food places. When he returned, he was carrying two cups and a little plastic shopping bag.

"Water, bandages, and lemonade." He knelt beside me.

"What good will all that do?"

He hooked his sunglasses over the neck of his t-shirt. Then he lifted the lid on the cup of water, put his hand under my knee, and poured the water over the wound. The water was warm, but it stung nonetheless. Still, I was impressed at the effort he'd made to get the water temperature right. I peered at him surreptitiously. His head was down, and the sun's rays glinted off shoulder-length hair so black it almost seemed blue. He wore it tied back in a ponytail, which looked natural, not phony and pretentious. At my firm a couple of investment bankers with receding hairlines had adopted the mini-ponytail look in some lame effort to compensate. On them, the effect was comical. Not on Evan though.

The hard lines of muscle in his shoulders and back flexed as he leaned forward and blotted at my knee. To my surprise, he used the hem of his olive green t-shirt to clean the wound.

"Oh, Evan, don't," I protested.

"It needs cleaning." He glanced up with a reassuring grin. His almond eyes were so black I couldn't even see the pupils. But his smile was so open and honest, like none of this was the least bit of trouble, and there was no place he'd rather be.

"This is an old shirt," he added. "From my Army days. It's seen worse than this. Anyway, time to let it go."

We both laughed, because when he laughed, I couldn't help but join him. His eyes gleamed, and little crinkly lines formed at their corners. How could a woman not want to laugh with him? No wonder Scott had blown a gasket last night when I'd said I was going running with Evan.

Scott and I considered ourselves engaged, even though no ring had ever been proffered. He was an immigration lawyer at Homeland Security, and he came from an uptight, politically well-connected Southern family. They didn't blow gaskets in Scott's family, so his display of temper had come across to me as almost flattering. Making Scott a little jealous was one thing, and not a very classy thing. But I knew it was about more than making an indifferent lover jealous. Scott wasn't even here to bait, yet I continued to sit, immensely enjoying the feel of Evan's hands all over my leg. Guilt fluttered at the base of my skull, like a moth trapped in a light.

Evan pulled a box of large bandages out of the little bag he'd brought with him.

"Where did you find those?" I peered over at the pavilion he'd just left. Baltimore's big tourist Mecca was full of overpriced chain restaurants and gift shops. No drugstores in a place like that.

"They have a security and first aid station. Any big mall does. People are always getting lost or injured or sick in malls, Sabrina. I went in, told them what happened, and asked if they had some first aid supplies. No big deal."

He shrugged in that mellow way he had. Everything about Evan as my personal trainer was like that—laid-back, low-key. He ripped open a packet of antibiotic cream and dabbed it all over my knee as I winced.

"That's what this is for." He handed me the lemonade. "To take your mind off the pain."

"I'm sorry I'm being such a girl," I said.

"I'm not." His voice sounded uncharacteristically husky. When his eyes tried to meet mine again, I looked away.

"I should go." I half-rose from the step, his hands still wrapped around my leg.

"Come on. First let me bandage this," he insisted.

I sat back down. He laid a piece of non-stick gauze against my knee before fixing the big square bandage on top. His hands were broad with long, thick fingers, and they moved with swift confidence, like he'd done this a million times.

"Were you ever a medical student or something?"

"Army medic."

That jarred me. How pathetic I must look complaining about my poor knee. But then he was younger than me, so he couldn't have been in for very long. Maybe he hadn't seen anything gruesome at all.

"Can you walk okay?" He rose with a lithe, animal grace and offered me his hand. As I took it, I realized I'd never remotely believed he was gay or bi. Except in a couple of really weird fantasies involving him and me and Matt Damon. I shook my head hard, trying to knock those embarrassing images out of my head.

"Does your head hurt?" Evan threw his arm around my shoulders, not in a romantic way, but like he was trying to steady me.

My head did hurt now, mostly because I'd shaken it so hard. I'd almost been able to hear marbles rattling around.

"It's fine." I squirmed out of his unexpected embrace.

"Where's your car?"

Normally I wouldn't even have my car with me. I can walk to my office from my condo at Harborview and usually do. But I'd driven to a client's that morning and then left my car in the office parking garage. When I told

Evan where I'd parked, he said that was a long walk with a sore leg, which it wasn't. Then he offered to come with me. I don't know why I said yes. Okay, I do know why I said yes. But at least I had the dignity to hesitate a bit.

We lumbered down the street side by side. By this time of the year, people usually needed to bundle up in heavy jackets, but the weathermen were calling it the warmest November on record. People in their business suits and designer dresses brushed past us, wrapped up in their cell phone conversations and oblivious to the warmth of the evening or the beauty of the Inner Harbor.

Yeah, the water was disgusting, but the place was picturesque in the extreme, something I'd only noticed around the time my hair started falling out.

I used to joke that with less weight on top of my head, I could think more clearly. During chemo I'd dug out my old sketchbooks and pastels, and on my good days, I'd come down and sketch the boats in the harbor or sketch the people strolling hand-in-hand around the promenade. At the time, I'd promised to spend more time on my art and less on adding up columns of numbers. As I walked with Evan, I realized it had been months since I'd taken time to do any sketching.

Evan interrupted my musings, laying a hand on the middle of my back as he guided me into the garage. We came to a halt in front of a bank of elevators.

I turned to face him. "I'm on the top level. Thanks for walking with me."

And then I kissed him, just like that—a shy little girl kind of kiss, a geeky peck on the cheek. I slapped a hand over my mouth.

He froze, his golden-brown skin darkening slightly. This would be the moment where he would tell me he had a girlfriend in L.A. or wherever he was from. A girlfriend way prettier than me, who didn't try to drop barbells on him or trip over her own shoelaces. He stared at me for the longest two seconds of my life.

"Hey, come on," I joked. "It wasn't that bad."

He gave a peculiar little smirk and turned away, planting his hands on his hips as if he were angry or thinking hard about something. I was fourteen the last time I'd tried to kiss a guy first, and it had gone about as well as this seemed to be going. I looked down at the grimy concrete floor and opened my mouth to apologize.

Evan spun around with a fluidity that startled me. He caught me by the elbow and pulled me close. He pressed his other hand against my neck, so that his fingers were tangled up in my hair and his thumb teased at the corner of my lips. Then he ducked his head down and kissed me, long and hard. My hands slipped around his back as if they were used to going there. I staggered a bit as his tongue slipped into my mouth. When we stopped for breath, he pressed his forehead against mine and sighed.

"That was incredibly unprofessional of me," he murmured.

He surprised me. I had suspected personal trainers were like tennis pros—that a fair percentage of them were in the job for the extracurricular benefits. I thought about Scott and how angry he'd been last night. He'd implied I was trying to bait Evan, and I'd denied it heatedly. Now here I was proving him correct. I've always hated women who try to make their boyfriends jealous. If a girl is that insecure about a guy, why not dump him? Why, indeed?

Years of accumulated stuff, inertia, the cowardly fear of an ugly scene, lack of confidence in her own attractiveness—that would be four answers right off the top of my head.

"I should really go. Now." The elevator doors opened and I felt a childish tear steal its way down my cheek.

"Hey," Evan protested softly.

He raised a hand again, as if he wanted to touch me. But then he drew it away, balled it into a tight fist, and clamped his other hand on top.

"I'm sorry," I babbled. "Scott and I had a fight yesterday, and he left for his business trip in a really bad mood. He was so flustered he even took the wrong damned laptop, which is not like him. He never lets me touch his computer. Barely lets it out of his sight. He's going to be in such a mess at his meeting in Mexico, and then he'll be in an even crankier mood when he calls later."

Behind me, the elevator doors whooshed closed again. Evan's face twisted, a deep line creasing his brow.

"Do you have the laptop with you?"

Talk about a non sequitur.

"What, when I go jogging I should bring someone else's computer? Not even my own?"

I laughed but he didn't. His whole demeanor had changed somehow, like a panther sighting a wounded rabbit.

"It's not in your car either?" He said it with a weird, disconcerting urgency.

"What do you care?" I was baffled and even a little alarmed. The kiss had obviously rattled us both way more than it should have.

"You know, I need to leave." I thrust out a hand to keep him at bay and backed up a little. What did I know about him, except he looked hot in a muscle shirt and could probably wrestle me into submission with frighteningly little effort? As I stepped away from him, two silver-haired businessmen approached the elevator and pressed the call button. The doors slid open again.

"Sabrina," Evan said. "Wait. I need to tell you something."

"Please don't."

I positioned myself close to the two, fatherly businessmen, who eyed the earring-wearing Hispanic with condescending sneers. One of them moved to block the center of the elevator doors. He pushed the "close" button before Evan could follow me.

I called Jess at the restaurant and told her I wouldn't be coming. I was tired and embarrassed, disgusted with my lame attempt at flirtation, and in a significant amount of pain. My knee had grown to the size of a grapefruit, and I worried something important might have been torn or damaged. I went home and put an icepack on it, reminding myself where I'd been one year ago. A pity party was better than no birthday party at all. I capped off the celebration with a glass of one of Scott's most expensive red wines. Scott fancied himself a bit of a gourmet cook and wine connoisseur. I didn't know enough about wines to know whether he was really an expert or just a poser—but I knew what I liked. So I had another glass. And then I had another. Soon I was feeling pleasantly drowsy.

I found myself in my mother's condo in Arizona. My father was there, which was strange since he'd never been near the place in real life. Weirder still, the two of them weren't trying to kill each other.

"Honestly, what kind of man misses his girlfriend's first post-cancer birthday?" My mother snapped as she set the table for dinner.

I muttered some half-hearted defense about how busy Scott was at work.

My father lifted a cup of coffee to his lips and slurped loudly.

Mom winced and frowned at him. "All I know is, Hugh would never do that to me."

Hugh was my stepfather, and the reason my parents' marriage had broken up.

"Honey, you need a new man." Mom waved a fork in my direction. "One that can make a commitment."

My father smirked at her. "You should talk about commitment."

God, even in my dreams they couldn't hold a civil conversation with one another.

"Oh, stop it," I said.

Just as things looked like they might escalate, my sister Angie walked into the room. As always, she was heavily pregnant.

"What about that guy from the gym?" she said.

My mother's eyes went wide with amazement. "Him? He's gorgeous! What would he want with her? Plus, he's a lot younger than her, and he's incredibly dangerous."

"Dangerous?" I repeated.

"You just have to look at him to know," my father piped up. "Looks like he probably deals drugs on the side, if you ask me."

"Well, you would know." My mother shot him her trademarked, condescending eye roll.

She put down a plate and turned her attention to me. "In any case, dear, that's not a recipe for a quiet life, is it? And you know that's what you need after the last couple of years—quiet."

"Hey." I started to splutter a protest, but she was right. I abandoned the effort and went back to her earlier remark. "Do you both really think he's dangerous?"

My father took a last gulp of coffee and stood to go. "All I'm saying is, remember what your old dad taught you about using a gun."

"Excuse me?"

My sister's cell phone had begun to ring. She dug it out of a diaper bag slung over her shoulder.

"Look, sis," she said to me. "I'm outta here. Dad just means, don't forget that thing about the trigger."

She wiggled her fingers at me and hurried out the front door.

"Trigger thing? What trigger thing?"

"Look, Kid, I'm sorry, but I have to go, too." My dad leaned across the table and gave me a quick peck on the cheek. Then he got up and headed out the door, too.

My mother went into the kitchen and turned a knob on the oven. Suddenly, she looked back at me and said, "For God's sake, Sabrina, don't step on the broken glass in your bare feet."

"Don't what?" I looked down at my favorite old brown loafers and then up at my mother again.

"Bare feet? What broken glass?"

The oven door gave a weird muffled thump as she threw it open.

I shook myself out of my confusion and discovered I was on the sofa in my own living room. I'd managed to down most of the bottle of wine and I had no idea what time it was. For a second, I thought Scott had come home. Maybe that thump had been him putting down his suitcase.

But no, he would be in Mexico for the rest of the week. I sat straight up on the couch and strained to hear any other sounds. There were none.

I told myself I was being crazy. Also, I needed to pee really, really badly. So I struggled to my feet and limped down the long corridor toward the bathroom. I saw a light where there should be none and stumbled into what I thought was my den. Unfortunately, I had stumbled into a whole new universe, one in which a man wearing a stocking over his face spun toward me, pointing a dark, shiny metal thing, and bellowed, "Get on the floor, bitch!"

I hope you enjoyed this excerpt of *Thirty-Nine, Again*.

A Note About the Author

Lynn Reynolds is a city girl trapped in Green Acres. She's a writer, wife and mom—although not necessarily in that order. Her short stories and poetry have been published in a few obscure literary magazines you've never heard of. In her previous life as a journalist, Lynn's feature articles appeared in major daily and weekly newspapers. Remember those?

At various times in her life, Lynn has been a child model, an actress, a stagehand, a secretary, a seller of ladies' lingerie and - in a brief fit of practicality, a computer programmer. Her secret ambition is to be a wench at The Renaissance Faire.

Contact info:
Lynn's website: www.lynnreynolds.com
Facebook: facebook.com/authorlynnreynolds